MORE ABOUT
THE AUTHOR

Tammy Hotsenpiller is a pastor, life coach, author, and speaker. As the founder and executive director of Women of Influence, a women's movement that educates, equips, and empowers women, Tammy has assisted numerous women in launching small businesses and following their dreams.

As a life coach she has coached CEOs of Fortune 500 companies and shared her wisdom on Fox and Friends, Fox News with Lauren Green, and contributed to Brooke Burke's *Modern Mom*. Tammy has previously published four books: *Taste of Humanity, 3 Skips and a Jump to Becoming a Woman of Influence, Curious, The Park*, and most recently *Collinsville*.

Tammy and her husband, Phil, live in Orange County, California, and adore their three amazing children, their equally incredible spouses, and six wonderful grandchildren.

PRAISE FOR
COLLINSVILLE

"*Collinsville* is a powerful story of how the Holy Spirit opens the eyes of our hearts to see people and situations that would otherwise go unseen. God awakens our hearts and minds through compassion and inspiration to participate with Him in ways He desperately wants to love and serve people in the world. Years ago, God showed me the elements of human trafficking and how to end it, which inspired the organization Saving Innocence to be birthed to help child victims escape in the United States. When God invites us into the story of redemption for the most vulnerable in our society we may never know the great impact that this has on the Kingdom, but I guarantee this adventure is one worth taking. I am hopeful that this book will ignite you to see where God is moving and how you can join Him in radically loving others."

— Kim Biddle, MSW, Founder and CEO, Saving Innocence

"*Collinsville* is a wonderful reminder of the need to truly engage the Holy Spirit for guidance in all aspects of life's journey. Tammy realistically captures the challenges many women face when juggling career, family decisions, and relationships and shows how walking in faith will bring light and clarity in times of darkness and uncertainty. It is uplifting and relatable."

— Carol Kurimsky, Fortune 500 Executive, Wife, and Mother

"The call to adopt takes us from the safe and ordinary to the supernatural, where complete dependence on our Heavenly Father through Holy Spirit is required in order to save a life and bring God's justice to a broken, hurting world. As *Collinsville* so aptly demonstrates, our Father's love guides us past all fear to accomplish His desire; to multiply, bring children into our hearts and homes, and love them as He loves us."

— Ted R. Youmans and Sheryl L. Youmans, Attorney at Law, authors, speakers, and Founders of FAMILYBUILDING, a Professional Law Corporation

"As a family that has adopted five boys, and with one biological daughter, we are so proud of Tammy for writing *Collinsville* and being an advocate for abused children. This book, we believe, will be used to educate and enlighten its readers!"

— Michael and Ivey Ketterer, adoptive parents

"Having personally worked in the legal field representing many families who have embraced adoption, and as an adoptive mother myself, I was truly moved by Tammy's powerful ability to inspire us to live by faith and seek a life-changing relationship with the Holy Spirit. *Collinsville* challenges you to boldly face your fears as you put your complete trust in God."

— Danielle Augustin, Esq., Speaker, Author & Founding Partner of OCKidsLaw.com

"For as long as I've known her, Tammy has had a heart for two things: serving God, and supporting women. Her ministry has spanned decades and continents as she's vivaciously dedicated herself to lifting other women up and advocating for causes that others have often overlooked. As a long-time advocate for those who've been exploited by human trafficking, it's poignant that Tammy would bring her gift for storytelling together with her activist heart in such a meaningful way. May this book speak to you, challenge you, and encourage you--just as Tammy has already done in the lives of so many."

— Allison Trowbridge, Author, *Twenty-Two*

"*Collinsville* tells a compelling story that highlights the very real and controversial issue of human trafficking. It's easy to think of human trafficking as a foreign issue that doesn't directly affect us, but as a Police Officer who has personally investigated human trafficking cases, I know it is a very tragic problem affecting the moral fibers of our society. *Collinsville* highlights how close this issue can hit to home and sheds light on how we can all play a part in ending it."

— Merisa Downs, Police Officer-Detective, Anaheim, California

Good and evil reside in our world and they
are forever vying for your attention.

COLLINSVILLE

 TAMMY HOTSENPILLER

COLLINSVILLE

by Tammy Hotsenpiller

First Edition, January 2018
Copyright © by Tammy Hotsenpiller

All rights reserved. Published by Influence Media
8163 E. Kaiser Blvd., Anaheim, CA 92808

ISBN: 978-0-9987293-3-6

www.tammyhotsenpiller.com

CONTENTS

This book is dedicated to Holy Spirit, the one that never leaves me nor forsakes me. You are, and always will be my light in dark places.

PREFACE

Our days are filled with spiritual warfare whether we see it or not. The enemy loves to bring discouragement and defeat into our daily activities and families.

As a child of God you have power over the darkness of the enemy. The problem comes when we focus more on the schemes of the enemy than we do the power of our God. The word of God is clear to say, "In this world you will have difficulty, but be of good cheer, for I have overcome the evil one." Pressure, deceit, confusion, temptation, and anger are all part of the Enemy's strategy to consume your attention. If Satan can capture your attention he will soon be directing your actions. God was aware we would do battle with the Enemy, so He equipped us with the perfect armor to win the war. Our job is to utilize the equipment He gave us.

In the book of Ephesians, 6:13 through 18, we read, *"Therefore put on the full armor of God, so that when the day of evil comes, you may be able to stand your ground, and after you have done everything, to stand. Stand firm then, with the belt of truth buckled around your waist, with the breastplate of righteousness in place, and with your feet fitted with the readiness that comes from the gospel of peace. In addition to all this, take up the shield of faith, with which you can extinguish all the flaming arrows of the evil one. Take the helmet of salvation and the sword of the Spirit, which is the word of God. And pray in the Spirit on all occasions with all kinds of prayers and requests. With this in mind, be alert and always keep on praying for all the Lord's people."*

Did you notice what the passage ends with? *"And always keep on praying."* Prayer is your point of power. This allows you to stay in communication with the Father and hear His words of love and direction for your life.

Let me encourage you to pursue the presence of Holy Spirit on a daily basis. Darkness turns to light when we proclaim the goodness of God. Speak it out over your daily affairs and see God begin to move in your midst.

Light and dark will always be a part of this world and it is up to us to decide which one we will follow. Our thoughts, actions, and words will determine our path. The beauty of a relationship with God is that we have the power to overcome the evil one. Remember the battle has already been won. Walk in your victory.

ACKNOWLEDGEMENTS

Thank you to my greatest champion and closest friend, my hubby. Phil, you have encouraged and supported me in every endeavor I have pursued. Thank you for believing in me. I love you.

Thank you to Lisa Haines, Marlene Tafoya, and Lori DeAngelo for the endless hours of reading, editing, and prayer over this manuscript. You are more than friends. You are co-laborers. I will forever love you all.

Thank you to Jessica Driskell, my assistant and friend. Watching you grow and develop into such an amazing woman has been a blessing to all that know you. Thank you for your endless love and support. You are one of a kind.

Thank you to Angie Mathews. You have a great way with words. Thank you for your assistance and creativity with *Collinsville*. You have a special gift and are a pleasure to work with.

Thank you to Simone Gabryk for the beautiful cover design for *Collinsville*. Your gift for detail and inspiration are truly ones to be admired.

Thank you to all the Women of Influence that have supported me in writing this book. Together we will tell our story and empower women for freedom, purpose, and the next generation.

And of course, thank you to my children who have always thought I could do anything.

P.S. Go for your dreams…I believe in you.

FOREWORD

"I love what you love. I am Holy Spirit." I remember the first time Tammy Hotsenpiller told me about her encounter with Holy Spirit in South Africa that eventually propelled her to write *The Park*. I remember her joyfully and reverently explaining how the Lord absolutely *loves* what we love.

At that time my toddler son was about to take his first little steps into preschool and I was a wreck. How could I let my sweet little baby go to preschool all day? Who would hug him if he scraped his knee? Who would notice all the small milestones he was meeting and celebrate them with excitement? I couldn't bear the thought of this little person potentially feeling alone, confused, or without comfort. But as I walked him to preschool that first morning the Lord reminded me of the words He had spoken to Tammy and was now speaking to me, "I love what you love." So, I let my baby go. I watched that precious boy walk into school filled with confidence that Holy Spirit loves what and whom I love, and I had peace. That peace allowed me to go and do what I was called to do without fearfully and anxiously worrying how my son was. His reassurance allowed me to feel confident that I was capable of being a good mom, a good wife, and a good television producer. The Lord loves what I love, so He will help me balance and care for all *my* loves.

Not long after that my husband and I began the journey of adoption. That is one of the many reasons *Collinsville* is so near and dear to my heart. Adoption is a life changing experience that cannot be highlighted or encouraged enough. All adoptive parents have different reasons for choosing adoption. My story is a little different from that of Rachel and Cody Brooks. My husband very much wanted a second child, but after a difficult bout with postpartum depression, pregnancy was not an option I was open to. So we considered adoption. I remember being a bit embarrassed to tell our adoption attorney why I was choosing adoption, but will never forget his response to my reason. "How do you know the Lord didn't allow you to suffer that difficult time so that your heart could be opened and softened to adoption?"

Although my reason for choosing adoption differs from that of Rachel and Cody Brooks, my experience with Holy Spirit is the same. There is no situation in my life where the Lord's protective providence hasn't been clearly evident. Tammy has captured this so beautifully in *Collinsville*. Through every twist and turn of our lives, on mountain tops and in dark places, Holy Spirit is ever present, always loving, and always available. He loves what we love. And, He loves us. Just like Rachel, we make it through with the help of Holy Spirit and we will make it through so much more with His divine support in the future.

Ashley Allen
Producer
NBC's America's Got Talent; ABC's The Bachelor, Bachelorette, and Dancing with the Stars; and FOX's Hell's Kitchen

CHAPTER ONE
MRS. BROOKS

Rachel resisted the temptation to race down Main Street squealing with excitement. She knew skipping wasn't exactly age appropriate for a freshly minted 27-year-old either. Forcing herself to, at the very least, wait until she reached the park's entrance, she took quick and deliberate steps towards her place of solitude and meditation, the park. It was her favorite place for speaking to Him.

The late summer sun dipped low on the horizon as she eagerly waited to cross the street and begin her divine conversation. There was so much to tell Him…so much to be grateful for.

Rachel was well aware she could speak with Him anywhere, anytime. He, Himself, had reminded her, *"I am with you always."* But there was just something about the time she spent with Him as she strolled the meandering pathways of Collinsville City Park that enabled her to feel closer to Him. Her prayer walks provided her the opportunity to truly express her gratitude, openly discuss her thoughts, penitently ask forgiveness, and humbly petition Him for her hopes and wishes.

He always responded. Maybe not how she expected or even how she wanted, but He always heard her and, whether she knew it or not, had already put a divine plan into action according to her needs.

Over the past six months her faith had grown exponentially. Receiving so many answers to prayers through unexpected events or people in ways that proved He knew not only her heart, but also exactly what would help her grow closer to Him and gain a greater understanding of His plan for her.

As she entered the park, a warm breeze brushed past her cheek and tossed her ponytail lovingly about. Holy Spirit was with her. The evening sounds of the cicadas chirping, frogs croakily singing and splashing on the lake, and the quiet whoosh of wind through the tall trees filled the otherwise silent evening. School had just started back up and even the warmth of an Indian summer couldn't keep many townspeople out past 7 p.m. on a Thursday. Taking a deep breath, she ruminated on the dinner she just came from. Love filled her so completely, she felt she needed to start talking immediately or her chest might burst.

It was the same feeling she had as a child when something wonderful happened at school and she would race home to tell her mom. Whether the news was about an award or an A-plus she'd achieved, Sarah would inevitably clap her hands in a round of applause fit for Beethoven and make it a night of celebration. Depending on their schedule, the fanfare would be followed by a special dinner out and a screening of a classic movie, or a fun night in, making her mom's special chocolate chip cookies while watching *Breakfast at Tiffany's*. Regardless, Sarah always made it a grand affair.

It was also like when Rachel would call Aunt Cali from NYU to share sweet details about a date with Tom, her first love, or a major success she'd had in her coursework. Aunt Cali's ever-present metal bangle bracelets would jingle wildly on the other end of the phone. It was always a surefire indication Cali was jumping and dancing around her kitchen. The physicality with which Cali joined in Rachel's excitement made any good news feel like something truly exceptional. Depending on the occasion, Rachel would sometimes discover a bouquet of brightly colored flowers or a ridiculous, animated e-card delivered shortly thereafter.

It was times like tonight when Rachel missed her mom and Aunt Cali more than ever. There were just certain accomplishments, relationships, prizes, and out of the ordinary events that called for cookies, flowers, old movies, silly e-cards, and the love of a mother and an aunt. However, now, knowing Holy Spirit intimately and having felt of His great love and compassion, she knew she had the champion of kings in her corner. Rachel experienced firsthand the depths of comfort and succor Holy Spirit provided in the midst of despair. She knew it was only through His influence that even when all else felt lost, there was still joy in Him.

The magical night and fun-filled week had left Rachel feeling emotionally spent, in a good way. It had also placed a spotlight on how much she missed the two most influential women in her life. She was eager to connect with Holy Spirit, her comforter, advocate, and friend. He always celebrated her wins. He was always there to soothe and encourage.

"Heavenly Father, I am so grateful...so grateful for so much. Thank you," she began, the words spilling from her lips so rapidly she feared being irreverent. Taking a deep breath even though she knew He understood her enthusiasm, she started again.

"Thank you so very much for all of the amazing blessings over the past year. Even through the loss of Aunt Cali, in the moments of my deepest grief, you were there to comfort me, alleviating the pain and helping me to have faith through the dark time. Your love ensured I didn't feel alone. I am so grateful for the knowledge of you, your atonement and sacrifice, and the ability to come to you through prayer. You know my heart, Dear Lord. Without me saying a single word, you already know. Thank you for blessing me with a renewed relationship with my dad. Thank you for his wife, Pam. Thank you for giving me a family when I thought I was all alone. Thank you for Collinsville and *Cali's*. I have found so much joy in running the cafe and boutique, and making a life here. But, most of all, thank you for Cody Brooks. Thank you for helping me to know my worth, giving me another chance at true love, and sending such a Godly, kindhearted man to be my partner in this life. I am so excited for our wedding on Saturday and can't thank you enough for where my life is currently. Thank you. In the name of Jesus Christ I pray, Amen."

A warm breeze swirled around Rachel. Like a divine hug as she closed her prayer, she twirled in the soft current of air and continued to ruminate on the week, still meditating, silently conversing with her Heavenly Father. Strolling along the park's manicured trail, taking in the lush foliage just beginning to show signs of autumn, she continued to discuss her heart with God, and bask in the love she carried from the groom's dinner.

Breaking with tradition, Cody and his grandparents held the rehearsal an afternoon early, leaving a day for final preparation (and eager anticipation) before the big wedding. They paid so much attention to detail. Rachel was blown away by their thoughtfulness and her husband-to-be's sweet sentimentality. Held on the charming patio of Collinsville's Italian culinary gem, *Francesco's*, the evening was filled with beautiful memories and a 10-course tasting menu that left Rachel feeling filled to the brim, both literally and figuratively.

They seemingly considered everything. At noon, Cody came to *Cali's* to pick Rachel up for a surprise picnic lunch. Taking her to the park, he guided her to the special tree where she had come to know Christ so many years before at Bible camp. Pulling out Grandma Benson's checkered tablecloth she and Cali used to use for their picnics, he laid out a gourmet lunch of beautiful hand-carved turkey sandwiches, roasted potatoes, and salad, all an ode to her simple childhood favorites.

Afterwards, they strolled over to check on the wedding location. As they approached the lake, Rachel could see the entire wedding party waving with enthusiasm armed with white balloons and little gifts. Susan and Pastor Bishop; Teresa, her husband Mike, and *baby* Izzy, who was no longer a baby, but quickly becoming a full-blown toddler; Rachel's dad and his wife Pam, and Cody's grandparents were all there clapping and congratulating the happy couple.

Cody's grandma, Hazel, had set out a lovely table of iced tea, lemonade, and little tea cakes that everyone, including baby Izzy, indulged in excitedly as Pastor Bishop led them in a run-through of the upcoming ceremony. Once they finished the rehearsal at the park, the wedding party made their way across the street to *Francesco's* where the chef surprised Rachel with Aunt Cali's famous sun-dried tomato risotto as the third course and her mom's chocolate chip cookies as part of dessert, even using an ice cream scoop the way her mom had to ensure the size was "as big as Rachel's head."

The nearly perfect day came on the heels of a week of birthday celebrations for Rachel's 27th. It all seemed to affirm she was in the right place with the right people. She had never felt so loved nor wanted to give so much love in return. As each wedding party member toasted the couple and made a sweet speech in their honor, Rachel couldn't help but want to return the favor.

"This day's about you and Cody," her dad had said with a laugh as she proceeded to offer complimentary speeches in response to everyone. "It comes with the territory of people celebrating you, princess. The opportunities are few and far between, so you might as well just grin and bear it. The next time will probably be at your baby shower."

"Dad!" Rachel had said blushing.

"Joe, you sure you're ready to be called *grandpa*?" Cody had asked laughing heartily. "I don't know if it fits your image."

"Aw," Pam had said patting Rachel's arm. "No rush, but I have to say, Joe and I were both ecstatic that you two didn't make us all wait through a long engagement. The prospect of having some little ones running around to cuddle and spoil, sooner than later, is very appealing."

"No pressure, of course," Joe had added with a crooked smile.

Now, back in the park walking with Holy Spirit she considered the future. Children were definitely on her mind, as well as Cody's. Together, they formed such a magical union, it felt only natural to build upon that love and create a family together. They had discussed the possibility of four kids, both desiring their future children to have something neither of them did: siblings, and quite a few at that.

Whether it was a way to help defend themselves, and their descendants, from ever feeling a level of abandonment and loneliness they had experienced in their own lives, or just a sincere desire to have a large brood, Cody and Rachel were eager to get married and get started.

***

The sun washed over Rachel's face as she squeezed her eyes shut tight. *Today's the day*, she thought. Her heart fluttered and she pulled her comforter up a bit higher, just enough to feel warm and snug, but not enough to block the pure morning light. She allowed her mind to fill with all of the things she was grateful for and began to silently list them off. *I'm grateful for my bed, this room, this house. I'm grateful for today, for Cody, for my family. I'm grateful for* Cali's Closet and Cafe, *the team there, and the amazing cinnamon rolls. I'm grateful for the Collinsville community, my friends, and our proximity to the city.* She continued, ticking off every single thing that came to mind that filled her heart with gratitude. Even things like a recent experience where she ended up owing a bit more in taxes than expected, but realized it was a good learning experience and could have been much worse.

As she began to slow, she bowed her head and segued into a formal prayer.

"Dear Heavenly Father, I am most grateful for your son, Jesus Christ. I am grateful for your sacrifice and His atonement. I am grateful for His teachings and example, and I'm grateful to know you and to have Holy Spirit as my guide, comforter, and closest friend. Amen."

Slowly opening her eyes, she reviewed her room. Her eyes immediately fell on the wall of family pictures and her heart momentarily lurched. Cali had hand-selected the collection of beautiful photographs highlighting Rachel's dearest people and places after her mom died. It was the first thing she saw when she arrived to live in Collinsville as a 14-year-old. There were photos of her and her mom in their New York City apartment, pictures of the city and all of the places that were the most precious to Rachel from her childhood.

When Aunt Cali passed away, Rachel inherited the house. She chose to stay in her old room as opposed to move into her dear aunt's personal space. However, she happily looted Cali's room for all of her best photographs and added them to her collage wall.

Now, on the morning of what some considered to be the most important day in a young woman's life, she had to admit she missed her mom and aunt. A soft breeze of pine-scented air wafted in through the open window and her own voice echoed in her mind, *"Thank you for blessing me with a renewed relationship with my dad. Thank you for his wife, Pam. Thank you for giving me a family when I thought I was all alone."*

She smiled sheepishly and turned from the picture wall to her mother's vintage wedding dress hanging gingerly from her vanity mirror. Suddenly she felt a warmth overcome her. Her ears burned with a sensation she had come to recognize as Holy Spirit and she knew in her heart, everyone would be witness to her special day, absolutely everyone.

She heard the doorbell ring and bounding out of bed she grabbed her robe and ran downstairs to meet Teresa and Maddy.

"Good morning, soon-to-be Mrs. Brooks!" Teresa exclaimed racing in with a giant box of donuts and bags draped down her arms filled with curling irons, flat irons, makeup brushes, and multiple bottles of hairspray. "How'd you sleep, girl? I was a wreck the entire week leading up to my wedding. You seem to be taking this all in stride, though."

"I couldn't be more excited about the wedding," Rachel said grabbing a French cruller. "I'm having to remind myself to enjoy everything leading up to it, because I'm just so ready to say our nuptials and be husband and wife. I've never been more confident in a major life decision."

"Oooh," Maddy cooed handing Rachel a cup of coffee from *Cali's*. "This is just like a fairytale. You're ruining my 'true love story' before it ever happens! There's no way it'll ever be this good."

They all laughed and Rachel took a big sip of coffee. "It's a beautiful day, right?" she asked, double-checking.

"Gorgeous," Teresa confirmed. "It's supposed to carry through the weekend and then they're saying possible first frost Monday. Fall is in the air! But, today, girl, it's still summer. It's your wedding and it's going to be spectacular."

"Let's get started?" Maddy asked pointing at the bags filled with beauty products.

With a nod Rachel agreed and took a bite of her donut. "I'm all yours, ladies. Just keep the caffeine and sugar coming. I need my physical energy to keep up with my internal excitement! I want to be completely and utterly in tune with today. I don't want to miss a thing."

***

Rachel remembered looking at photographs of her mom on her wedding day. In addition to hearing stories about Papa and Mama D'Angelo's emigration from Italy, looking at her mom's old wedding photos was a favorite pastime as a child. Sarah was beautiful. Rachel wasn't being biased or clouded by fond memories of her mother; Sarah looked like a movie star. Based on looks alone, she should have *been* a movie star.

Married when she was only 19, Sarah wore an Audrey Hepburn style 1960's vintage dress she found at a secondhand store on Manhattan's upper west side. An ivory silk tea length gown with a sweetheart bodice and a lace overlay, it was classic, beautiful, and perfect. Perfect for her mom's wedding at the Long Island Country Club in 1989; and perfect for Rachel's afternoon wedding in the park today.

Staring at the dress as Teresa shoved a few more bobby pins into the back of her hair, Rachel wondered if her feelings for Cody were the same as Sarah's for Joe, Rachel's dad. Sarah had once told Rachel the story about how their relationship dissolved, going from something passionate and magical to something claustrophobic and toxic. Could that happen with her and Cody, she wondered? Was she being naive to think that he was *the one*?

Suddenly her heart began to race as a thick cloud of hairspray filled the room. Rachel could feel her fingers involuntarily tighten around the armrests of the chair. Feeling her death grip constrict as it became difficult to get a fresh breath of air, she pursed her lips and closed her eyes. Saying a silent prayer in her heart, petitioning the Lord for confirmation that marrying Cody was the right thing, she waited.

She could hear her friends chatting in the background, but it was hollow and muddy, difficult to make out, as if she was underwater. She worked to tune-in to her heart. Softly, a still, small voice answered deep from within her chest and bubbled up to her ears. *You already know, my love.*

The wave of anxiety subsided and Rachel began to giggle. It was one of the sweetest ways the Spirit had ever spoken to her heart. In a way, it felt like a gentle rebuke for even questioning it.

Maddy and Teresa both stopped what they were doing and looked at Rachel with curiosity.

"What'd we miss?" Teresa asked.

Rachel just smiled, feeling her cheeks turn pink. "Can I see yet?" she asked, eager to see her hair and makeup.

"Not yet," Teresa said. "Maddy, hand me the hair comb?"

Maddy pulled out a black velvet box and handed it to Teresa. "It was my grandma's," she said with a wink. "This will be your *something borrowed*."

Opening the box, Rachel found a beautiful crystal and pearl emblazoned vintage silver hair comb shaped like a butterfly. "It's stunning," she said, running her fingers over the delicate filigree.

"It reminded me of the necklace you wear sometimes," Teresa said, pushing the comb into place and securing it with a few more bobby pins.

Rachel put her hand to her neck where the butterfly charm from her Aunt Cali occasionally sat. A gift for her seventh birthday, it was to inspire and give hope after her dad left. *The butterfly symbolizes hope and renewal*, she could hear her aunt saying. *Change can be hard, but good.*

"It's absolutely perfect," Rachel said. "Thank you, both, for everything."

"You may want to have one of us help you pull down your hair tonight," Maddy said laughing. "It's not coming down on its own! And, while I know Cody's good with his hands, I'm not sure that's how you'll want to spend your wedding night."

They all agreed with a chuckle and then Teresa walked to the vanity to get the dress. "Okay, my dear. It's time."

"Really? Already?" Rachel asked surprised. "What time is it?"

"Showtime," Maddy replied.

Standing, Rachel took the gown and held it to her chest with excitement. Pulling it on, she turned around and let

Maddy help close the back.

"I'm dying to see my hair and face," Rachel said, bouncing impatiently as Maddy struggled to button the dress. "It's terrible making me wait to see what you've done."

As Maddy secured the final button, Teresa took Rachel by the shoulders and led her down the hall to the full-length mirror in Cali's old room. Newly redecorated, it was going to be Cody and Rachel's room starting tonight. Rachel was still getting used to it and was momentarily distracted as the girls posed her in front of the mirror.

"Well?" Maddy prompted.

Focusing, Rachel gazed into the mirror trying to register what she was seeing. Squinting, she looked at the woman before her. It looked like her mom, only with brown hair. Stepping a little closer, she touched her reflection and smiled.

"You're stunning," Teresa said, wrapping her arms around her shoulders.

"You look like a model," Maddy agreed. "Like a bride that should be in a magazine."

"Ahhh! You guys, I'm getting married today!" Rachel exclaimed coming to her senses.

Maddy joined the girls for a group hug. Then, grabbing Rachel's hands, they all danced around the room screaming and giggling until they collapsed onto the floor with an excited, collective sigh.

"You weren't joking about my hair," Rachel said. "I don't think it moved."

"It's all about the proper hairspray to bobby pin ratio," Teresa said with a wink. "Let's g-g-g-g-Go!"

***

Celia met the trio at the park's entrance. On Sundays she was the executive producer at Collinsville Community Church ensuring the key message, music, and media all came together without a hitch. The rest of the week, she worked as a successful wedding planner, often traveling to the city to create beautiful, high price tag celebrations. As her gift to Rachel and Cody, a beloved couple in the community, she was coordinating their wedding, making everything run smoothly.

"My heavens!" she exclaimed as the girls approached. "You're quite a vision. Cody's going to flip."

Rachel blushed. "Thanks, Celia. Did you see him? How's he doing? Did he seem nervous?"

"He seemed over-the-moon. He's so eager to see you. Everyone is. All the guests have arrived and are now seated. We can start whenever you're ready."

Rachel turned to look at her friends. In their berry-colored dresses and matching lipstick, they both looked exuberant and lovely. "I'm ready. How about you, ladies?"

"We got this, girl!" Teresa exclaimed, patting Rachel's hand with excitement.

Celia got on her walky-talky and let her team know the women were heading in.

Entering the park, Rachel felt as if every follicle on her body was electrified. Goosebumps, what she learned from her Aunt Cali to call *God bumps*, covered her arms and the earth beneath her feet was suddenly buoyant, making it feel like she was walking on clouds.

As they approached the starting point, Rachel could see her dad holding baby Izzy's hand. He looked as if he could be part of Frank Sinatra's Rat Pack in his classic black tuxedo. It made Rachel's heart leap to see him so comfortable with the toddler. She remembered what a fun dad he was when she was little. He was her knight in shining armor, until she got a little older and was able to begin seeing some chinks in that armor. Thinking about how far her dad had come, she looked forward to him being a great man for her kids. The man he was unable to be for her.

When they were close enough, he let go of Izzy's hand and she ran to her mom.

"Wow, princess, you look so much like your mom," Joe

said, taking a pause. "She'd be so happy for you." He wiped at a stray tear with a handkerchief and shoved it back in his pocket.

"She *is* happy for me," Rachel whispered giving him a kiss on the cheek. "She's here with Auntie Cali. Can you feel it? Papa and Mama. They're all here."

He smiled and cocked his head. "I knew something felt exceptional about today."

Rachel knew Cody was already standing at the altar with Pastor Bishop and his best man, Mike, Teresa's husband. She strained to see the guests, the arrangement, and her soon-to-be husband, but blocked by trees, she relaxed and decided she'd just have to enjoy the surprise. Celia's assistant, Regina, waved her hands, letting the small group know it was time to head down the aisle.

Classical music started and Maddy started the procession, then Teresa and Izzy holding hands made their way forward, Teresa prompting Izzy every couple of feet to toss petals on the ground from her little basket. Suddenly the music changed and Joe gave Rachel's hand a soft squeeze.

"Here we go, princess."

Rachel took a deep breath in and determined to not let it out until she made eye contact with Cody. Her feet felt like they were floating just above the petal-laden ground. As she took each bouncy step forward, her heart jumped with glee. She half expected to hear a *boing* every time she lifted a foot.

As she turned the corner, gripping her dad's hand, she was struck by large, vibrant bouquets of flowers and beautiful silk fabrics swaying in the breeze forming an ethereal outdoor space. The many guests, seemingly all of Collinsville, were all turned looking at her.

Then, just a few feet past the front row stood Cody. His eyes twinkled as they locked with hers. His sweet, dimpled grin was as big as she'd ever seen it. Her heart swooned and she thought there was a very real chance she was unwittingly dancing as she reached him. She wanted to grab his hands and hop around wildly like she had done with the girls just a short while before. Deciding it was inappropriate, she simply mouthed *I love you.*

"Who presents this woman to be married to this man?" Pastor Bishop asked ceremonially.

"Her mother and I do," Joe said.

Rachel's heart skipped a beat and she squeezed her dad's hand tighter in appreciation. She felt in her bones it was true. Her mom was watching over her. A warm breeze rustled the trees, lifting the silk panels in a delicate dance, and Rachel knew Holy Spirit was there. Joe patted Rachel's hand and then placed it in Cody's.

"I love you, princess," he said giving her a kiss on the cheek.

"Love you too, dad."

Having decided to go traditional and stick with the classic vows, Rachel and Cody were able to follow Pastor Bishop's lead, relax, listen, and enjoy the ceremony along with everyone else.

"I, Rachel, take you, Cody, for my lawful husband…," Rachel repeated, following Pastor Bishop's prompting.

"To have and to hold from this day forward, for better, for worse, for richer, for poorer…," she continued. Her hands were vibrating with earnestness as she looked into his eyes. No matter what, they were in this life together, she thought; from this day forward they were a team.

"In sickness and health, until death do us part," she finished, as Cody carefully wiped a tear from the corner of her eye, protecting her makeup.

Pastor Bishop stepped towards them. "Collinsville, it's my sincere pleasure," he announced, wrapping his arms around both of their shoulders, "to pronounce this beautiful, young couple as Mr. and Mrs. Cody Brooks! Cody, go on and kiss that girl!"

The guests erupted in a round of applause as Cody leaned in and gently cradled Rachel's face in his strong hands. Pausing a moment, he gazed into her eyes. It was as if he were etching the moment into his memory for all eternity, and in turn engraving it in hers as well.

"I love you, Mrs. Brooks," he said softly. Then, embracing her fully he gave her a tender kiss. The sensation that started in Rachel's chest and flowed through her body was electric. As she and Cody solidified their union, she could feel her heart and soul expanding, doubling, as they were no longer independent of one another, but joined as one.

CHAPTER TWO
LITTLE ONES TO HIM BELONG

Rachel's knees hurt. She'd been on them a lot in prayer the past month. Today, as she pulled herself up from the hard, wooden floor, she vowed to order a kneeling pad or cushion. Glancing in the mirror it was obvious she'd been crying. Cody, as well as everyone else, would be able to tell. *Makeup*, she thought. *Lot's of it.*

Grabbing her makeup bag, she meticulously layered on cover-up until she buried the blotchy redness. Adding a classic cat eye with two thick swipes of eyeliner, she felt sufficiently covered up. She took a deep breath, gathered her things, and headed down to meet Cody.

"All set," she said reaching the bottom of the stairs. "Sorry I took so long."

Setting down the book he'd been reading as he patiently waited for her, he looked up and smiled. "Going somewhere special?"

She laughed sheepishly. "Just felt like I needed some color. Have you seen my sunglasses?" she asked, digging through her purse.

He walked over to her and wrapped his arms around her shoulders. Giving her a sweet kiss on her forehead he replied, "I have not. It's snowing and cloudy outside, Rach. Why are you hiding?"

She felt a wave of emotion erupt from her core. Even with all of the hardship and loss she had experienced over the years, the dark loneliness she was once familiar with, nothing fit the definition of gut-wrenching more than this. There was nothing she could do to control it. A sour bitterness flooded her body overwhelming her sense of reason and suddenly a gush of ugly tears poured from her eyes. Eyeliner stained droplets hit Cody's hands as he tried to gently wipe the tears away. But, it was like having windshield wipers while driving into a monsoon. His thumbs weren't helping.

"Uugghh," she wailed. Half laughing, half sobbing, she added, "I thought I'd gotten this all out. I'm sorry, Cody. I'm like a crazy person. I don't know what's happening to me."

"What's this about?" he asked, his brow furrowed with concern.

"It's nothing. It's stupid. I'm completely overreacting, and I know it. But, I have no control," she said, blowing her nose.

"Rach," he pleaded. "Talk to me."

"I got my period again," she said, defeated. "I know it's only been six months, and some people try for years, but I didn't expect this. I believed getting pregnant would be easy for us. I don't understand why it's not happening."

Cody stroked her hair as she hid her face in his chest.

"It's totally TMI, but even before we got married I was charting my cycle and using a fertility indicator to know when the best time was to conceive," she said with an embarrassed laugh. "You know, I like to plot and plan, and have control. My prayer walks have been so quiet. I haven't heard Holy Spirit. I've been spending every free moment on my knees upstairs, just trying to talk to Him. Plead my case. But, this isn't one of my real estate law disputes. I don't have control over this."

"Aw, Rach. Why have you waited so long to talk to me? I don't ever want you feeling like you've got to carry a burden like this on your own," he said. "We're in this together. I mean, maybe it's me. Maybe I need to be doing something differently or getting tested, right?"

Rachel lifted her face to look into his eyes. "It's terribly unromantic to talk about this stuff. We're still newlyweds . It seems ridiculous to be so upset, so early. I just didn't want to bother you."

"This is our family we're talking about. We're both eager to get started. I'm well aware babies aren't brought by a stork. The things involved in baby making don't make me squeamish or detour me from how madly in love with you I am. If anything, it draws me closer to you and makes our love seem even larger," he said, giving her a kiss on the lips. "Totally romantic in my opinion."

Rachel lifted herself up from Cody's embrace and smiled with relief. "You're the answer to my prayers in so many ways. But today, at this moment, Holy Spirit is answering my freak-out through you and I am so grateful. So blessed."

"We'll get through this," Cody reiterated. "Kids are in our future, even if they don't happen exactly as planned."

Rachel stepped into the hallway bathroom to rinse her face. "Are you really open to getting checked?" she asked peeking back out. "I'd like for us both to talk to a professional. Just to see."

"Absolutely," he agreed. "I'll make an appointment for us to see Dr. Dave."

***

Rachel picked up a magazine from the coffee table and thumbed through as they waited. She could hear the girls at the front counter talking about what to do for lunch. For a moment it made her angry that they'd be discussing something so insignificant at a time like this. *What was keeping Dr. Dave?* she wondered.

"Relax," Cody said, putting a hand on her thigh stopping her from bouncing her leg erratically.

"Do you think they know why we're here?" she asked.

"Who? The office assistants?" he asked. "Maybe. I had to give some information when I called to make the appointment. Why?"

"It's embarrassing," she said, sinking in her chair.

"It's normal," Cody said, reassuringly. "I can think of a lot of other reasons to see a doctor that would actually be embarrassing."

"But, it's like we're incapable of doing something even cavemen were able to do. I feel stupid."

"Rach, we've got the mechanics," Cody said with a laugh. "There may just be something chemical or hormonal off. We're not stupid. We're victims of our circumstance."

She nodded, knowing he was right and tried to get her emotions to catch up with her head. After spending the morning reading online about the various ways male and female fertility specimens were collected, Rachel was already feeling sullied and discombobulated. Without having even spoken to the doctor she was considering what she was and was not comfortable with.

"Maybe it's a sign?" she asked. "Maybe we're not supposed to have kids of our own. Do you think we should be involving medical intervention?"

"This is a conversation we can have once we know what we're dealing with," Cody responded. "We're just here to gain some additional insight."

"But, the…," Rachel started.

"Mr. and Mrs. Brooks?" one of the girls at the front desk called.

Rachel gave Cody an uneasy look and he squeezed her hand with reassurance as they were guided to Dr. Dave's office.

A small-town doctor, he was what you would expect in some regards, and not so much in others. Exceptionally qualified, he graduated in 1965 from Stanford's School of Medicine and after treating veterans returning from Vietnam at the San Francisco VA Medical Center for a number of years, he decided to join Doctors Without Borders, which at the time was brand new. After years of working with those in desperate need around the world, he retired to Upstate New York. He had fallen in love with Collinsville, Cheesecake Yogurt, and Collinsville Community Church on a vacation with his wife. When friendly gestures to treat friends and church members' occasional ailments evolved into house calls multiple times a week, he decided to open an official practice.

In his mid 70's, he was what he liked to call *experienced* in most medical matters, but not opposed to hearing what patients had discovered through late night Internet searches. He endeared himself to Rachel forever when he offered to read a new study she'd found about adrenal fatigue, which he was not familiar with. After comparing notes, they concluded she was just tired and needed to get more sleep.

While she really liked Dr. Dave, Rachel had never gone to him for anything beyond an eye infection or sleep issues. She wasn't sure how she felt about having him perform a pap smear or the like. Taking a seat next to Cody in matching high back leather chairs, she reviewed the many pictures on his desk taken in exotic places.

"Dr. Dave will be with you in just a moment," the assistant said with a nod. "For cases like yours, he likes to just talk things out before making any recommendations or requiring any specimen collection."

Rachel felt her stomach twist and she shifted uneasily in her seat.

Cody knowingly patted her hand. "He's just going to make sure we have the mechanics right," he teased.

Just as the assistant left, Dr. Dave made his way in.

"Hello, my friends," he greeted them, shaking both of their hands before taking a seat at his desk across from them. "We're looking to make one plus one equal three, huh?"

"Pretty much," Cody replied. "Seems our math isn't adding up yet."

Dr. Dave leaned forward and rested his forearms on the

desk. Pulling his glasses down to the tip of his nose so he could look them both squarely in the eyes, he said, "Well, let's chat then."

***

"You okay?" Cody asked on the drive home.

"Sure," Rachel replied. "Just thinking about everything. I'm torn between being grateful for modern medicine, happy to have Dr. Dave's help in determining why we haven't been successful, and feeling disappointed we have to involve other people. It's such a personal, intimate thing."

"I understand," Cody said. "Let's stick with gratitude."

Rachel nodded in agreement. "I'm also thinking ahead. What if something's wrong? What if we really can't get pregnant without some sort of medical intervention? I'm not sure how I feel about most of the options."

Cody was quiet for a moment. "It's completely our choice," he replied. "No one's going to make us do anything we don't want to do. And, honestly, I'm going to let you take the lead on a lot of this. So much of it revolves around your body, I want you to be completely on board with anything and everything we try."

As they pulled down the long driveway to the garage, Cody stopped the car to look Rachel in the eyes. "I love you. There are so many ways to respond to this challenge, so many options. We'll do what's right for us," he said. "I'm open. I love the idea of adopting, if we need to."

Rachel shifted at the mention of adoption. "I don't know," she said, playing with her scarf. "It makes me uncomfortable."

***

It was the perfect day at *Cali's Closet and Cafe*. Mid-March, the soft, early spring sunshine offered just enough heat to gently defrost and bring to life all of Collinsville. Chilly enough outside for a light jacket and cozy sweater; inside the music was swinging, friends were chatting, milk was steaming, and pastries were baking. The positive energy, lighthearted conversations, and sweet scents mingled for a completely enchanting morning.

Rachel made her way around the cafe greeting customers and checking in with friends. Having received a diagnosis of polycystic ovarian syndrome, PCOS, Rachel was feeling focused. She liked understanding what was wrong and knowing what her options were. Over the years, she had just assumed missed periods were a result of stress. With her mom dying when she was only 14, women's health was a conversation somewhat skimmed over with Aunt Cali. Dr. Dave suggested more blood work and starting Clomid as a fertility treatment.

The blue skies had Rachel eager for a prayer walk. It seemed pregnancy success rates were decent for women with PCOS on Clomid and she was filled with hope and faith that everything was going to work out. She had also discovered a number of women online touting the negative effects of caffeine and sugar for those with the ovarian syndrome. She was just rounding the corner of a difficult caffeine and sugar detox week and feeling good.

Chatting with a couple of *Cali* regulars about the Collinsville Community Church band and their upcoming special performance, Rachel noticed Teresa walk through the door with Baby Izzy in tow. Instantly Rachel's mood darkened. She felt like a ripe banana someone forgot in a hot car, just sitting and blackening in the sun without any ability to stop it. Looking for an escape, she quickly excused herself from the couple and made her way toward the cafe's counter.

"Rach!" Teresa exclaimed catching her in the middle of the floor before she could hide. "Long time no see, friend. How are you?"

"Well, hi there! I'm good," Rachel stammered feeling awkward and standoffish. "How are you ladies?"

"I miss you," Teresa said. "Mike and I were just talking

about how long it's been since we've all done dinner and I decided I needed a decaf coffee and some Rachel time. So, here we are. Do you have a bit to hang out?"

"Oh, I know. It's been too long," she replied. "Gosh, you're getting so big, sweet girl."

Teresa broke out in laughter. "Are you talking to me or Izzy?" she asked, patting her very pregnant belly.

Rachel bristled at the motion. It felt as if Teresa was purposefully rubbing it in her face. And, while she knew that was crazy and in no way what was actually happening, her body was physically reacting to the negative scenario in her mind. The heat rising from her neck was certainly turning her cheeks pink.

Rachel's inability to get pregnant was inadvertently turning her into the epitome of a hater. The exact opposite of what she was striving to be. She hated that she was having a visceral, spiteful reaction to her friend.

"You know, I forgot, I have to call in a couple of orders. Most of our vendors close early on Friday's, so I need to hurry. I'm sorry," Rachel said, turning to head to the backroom.

"Okay," Teresa said disappointed. "Real quick, did you get the invite? For the baby shower? My mom said you haven't RSVP'd yet."

"Oh," Rachel replied feeling unable to muster anything else with the giant ball that was welling up in her throat. She felt trapped and was afraid she could burst out crying at any moment. "Of course I'll be there. Tell your mom I'm sorry for not replying."

Teresa lit up with relief. "Woot, woot!" she said. "All right, well, if we don't see you before, see you Saturday at 11 a.m. Say goodbye to Auntie Rachel, Izzy."

The adorable toddler, who Rachel found herself barely able to look at without breaking into an uncontrollable sob fest, placed her pudgy little hand against her lips and blew

Rachel a big kiss. "Bye-bye," she said waiving wildly in the air.

"Bye, Rachel. Good luck with all the orders," Teresa said, grabbing her in an embrace.

The wave of tears was forming. It was as if Rachel could visually see the swell before it even physically manifested in her gut. The sensation of Teresa's beautifully round belly, filled with life, pressed against her own vacant core was too much. Gritting her teeth and flashing a good-bye smile, Rachel dashed to the backroom. Making it to her office just in time to bury her face in her hands, she cried unable to control her breath. It all just seemed so unfair.

Struggling to not take it personally, to understand why it wasn't happening for her, she said a silent prayer. Frantic, unable to calm down, the divine plea came out deranged and chaotic. Unsure of whether to ask for guidance, patience, or peace, in a moment of clarity she heard herself and realized she was no longer praying. *No wonder I haven't been able to hear Holy Spirit*, she thought, her breath slowing. Her conversations with God had been reduced to a one-sided temper tantrum demanding a baby.

Realizing her error and ashamed by her monomaniacal behavior, Rachel took in deep, calming breaths and worked to slow her mind. She couldn't believe how wrapped up she'd become in herself and her own desires. It was like nothing she'd ever experienced, there was something primal about it.

A song she hadn't sung since she was a child came to mind and she softly began to hum the first verse, recalling the lyrics. *Little ones to Him belong. They are weak, but He is strong.*

"Yes, Jesus loves me," she reminded herself.

Finally calm, she grabbed her things and snuck out *Cali's* backdoor. She needed to get to the park. As she hurried down Main Street, she made an effort for the first time in months to acknowledge the world around her. Waiving at familiar faces

46

as they passed, she took in the early spring beauty of Collinsville. The blue skies, verdant tree-lined streets, crisp, fresh air all culminated to nurture her soul as she approached Collinsville Community Park.

She thought about her mom and Aunt Cali, the two beautiful parental figures in her life. Feeling a pang of sadness, she wished they were here. Rachel envisioned them snuggling close together by a fire in Cali's backyard, the three stooges, discussing and weighing her fertility options. Their discordant, yet altruistic, support of Rachel bringing fresh perspective, as well as comedic relief, as they debated the best way to approach the difficult process. Her heart yearned for their maternal guidance — a *mother's love*.

A mother's love, Rachel thought. Her mom, Sarah, struggled in life, but never as a loving mother. One thing Rachel never had to question was whether or not she was loved. Partly because of Aunt Cali, she reminded herself. When Sarah was unable to be present, Cali seamlessly picked up the slack. Cali's love for Rachel was so pure. As her aunt she wasn't required to show up or fix things, but she always did; and with such flair and style.

Rachel smiled thinking about her Auntie Cali. When Sarah died, Rachel didn't wonder for a moment what would happen to her. While she mourned her mother's loss, she never had the added stress of worrying about where she would end up. Cali's love was so strong, so mother-like, Rachel felt protected and nurtured even through the loss of her mom. They were both amazing women in Rachel's mind because they loved her unconditionally, regardless of their title of mom or aunt.

"Oh mom, Auntie Cali, I miss you both so much," Rachel said softly. A soft chill caused *God bumps* to erupt down her arms. "Mom, even when things were not stable or comfortable for you, you were able to make me feel loved. I wish I had your beautiful take on things now; only you'd be able to make this whole process charming and somehow romantic. And, Aunt Cali, when you had the freedom to do anything, you chose to give of yourself to ensure I was taken care of. I wish I had your unfettered approach combined with your faith. If only I could accept everything with a heart of gratitude like you did."

Talk to Heavenly Father, her heart replied.

As she passed through the gate to the park, almost instantly she felt a sense of peace wash over her. Softening her heart, humbling her spirit, Rachel stepped onto her favorite path and bowed her head.

"Dear Heavenly Father," she began. "I've lost myself to baby mania. Please forgive me for my demanding behavior. My personal desires have consumed me and made me lose track of everything else in my life. I've forgotten to love and care for those around me. I haven't even been able to celebrate Teresa's pregnancy because of my jealousy. I'm filled with envy. It's a terrible feeling and has taken over my thoughts and feelings towards others. I feel so out of control, I'm not even sure what I need to pray for. You know I desire to get pregnant and start a family, but please help me find a sense of peace through the process. Heavenly Father, please don't let these feelings undermine my faith. Please help me to not lose sight of me. Allow me the ability to be happy for others. And, if needed, please open my heart to alternative options. Lastly, please bless me with the guidance of Holy Spirit. Allow me to know with clarity which path is best for our family. In Jesus name, Amen."

Closing her prayer, Rachel stopped and looked up. She found herself under the tree where she had accepted Christ into her heart years before. She recalled how young she had been. As a soft spring breeze blew past, cooling her tear-worn cheeks, she reflected on the many changes and seemingly impossible things that had happened since then.

A few years after Bible camp, her mom would die. And,

rather than lose all hope, Rachel would find a new life with Aunt Cali in Collinsville. Aunt Cali, who, without question, took her in as her own.

Rachel would go on to attend NYU and become a successful New York lawyer.

Then Rachel would struggle through the loss of Aunt Cali, her only remaining family at the time. It was only through the tender mercies of Heavenly Father that she was able to gain a personal relationship with Holy Spirit, find happiness, love, family and home again. To think, during the overwhelming time of personal hardship that she would reconnect and have a thriving relationship with her dad, fall in love with Cody, find a life and inherit a successful boutique and cafe in Collinsville, would have been like believing in fairy tales.

But, here she was. By the divine grace and the love of Heavenly Father, she had made it through impossible challenges.

We will get through this, too, a still, small voice rose from her heart. Relieved, excited, and eager to hear more, Rachel took a seat on a nearby bench and waited. Holy Spirit was talking to her and she was going to listen. After a few deafening beats, He continued.

Rachel, I love you. I love what you love. I want for you to have joy. I want for all my children to have joy. A family is paramount to my plan for you, for everyone. Be open and be patient, but most of all, continue to walk in faith.

Rachel's face felt flushed and her ears began to ring as if she'd just heard a loud shot. An overwhelming sense of peace enveloped her and she felt divinely loved. His words echoed in her heart and she worked diligently to commit the heavenly guidance to mortal memory.

"Thank you," she whispered.

She couldn't get to Cody quick enough. Running to his workshop just a few blocks away, she paused at the open door to compose herself. She could see him working on a custom hutch a couple from Manhattan had commissioned. Covered in sawdust and moving with graceful, deliberate strokes he looked like a character out of a romance novel. Rachel giggled as she approached. Cody set down his sander and leaned forward to give her a kiss. After reciprocating, she dipped down and nestled into his dusty chest.

"What brought about this pleasant surprise? I didn't think I'd see you until later tonight," he said, wrapping his arms around her.

"I finally heard from Holy Spirit," she said excitedly.

Cody loosened his embrace and smiled. Rachel felt butterflies as he looked at her recognizing the magnitude. She loved that he understood. Having his own relationship with Holy Spirit, Cody knew the subtle ways in which He offered comfort, guidance, and love; and she loved that Cody got it.

"I'm so glad, Rach. How do you feel?"

"For context, I should explain how I was feeling before," she replied. "I woke-up feeling pretty good today, but by mid-morning I found myself in a completely dark place. Teresa and Izzy stopped by, and seeing her so pregnant and happy, made me bitter and spiteful. I was so awful. I could barely be cordial. It was terrible, Cody," she said, pausing for a moment to breathe and suppress the quickly building pressure of unshed tears.

Composed, she continued, "After they left, I just disintegrated. I felt horrible for being so malevolent. I felt horrible for being so wrapped up in myself and my desires. And, I felt sorry for myself, too. It was just bad. By the grace of God, I found my way to the park for a prayer walk. It was the first one I'd been on in a long time. I don't know if it's because of the wintery weather or my cold mental state, but I've been blocked mentally, spiritually, and physically. I'd been relying on my bedside prayers. Being out in the park seemed to get *me* out of my own way, allowing me to be still, listen to my heart, and hear Him."

"That's awesome," Cody said giving her another hug. "I can completely relate. Most of the time it's me causing any hold-ups in the dialogue. He is always there, ready to talk. It's just a matter of when I'm ready, and able, to listen."

Rachel nodded. Then, unable to stall the impending tears any longer, she grabbed a paper towel and softly dabbed at her eyes.

"Cody, I want to keep trying, but I think we should look into adoption."

"Really?" he asked, surprised.

"Yeah. I don't know why I was ever opposed to it," she replied. "I mean, how closed-minded of me. Especially when I was selflessly taken in by Aunt Cali and you were raised by your grandparents. They weren't just guardians, they were our parents, our mothers and fathers, regardless of whether they physically delivered us. Holy Spirit reminded me, Heavenly Father wants all of His children to experience joy in this life. If we could have a family and provide a loving, nurturing home to one of God's children who may not otherwise get that, why wouldn't we? It's like a twofer."

Laughing softly through her tears of revelation, she added, "I've been resistant to the idea mainly because I had this romanticized view of what having a baby was supposed to look like. We're already way outside that frame of view, so let's start looking into it."

CHAPTER THREE
ADOPTION

Brimming with love and gratitude, Rachel felt confident in her decision. In lieu of a growing baby in her belly, she was feeling pregnant with anticipation. Once again comfortable in her own skin, her hope for the future had returned and the single-minded obsession with getting pregnant had subsided. There was something about having a clear agenda and a revised plan that allowed her the space to breathe and see clearly.

Cody noticed the change right away. He shared his gratitude for Rachel's heartache being lifted in their first family prayer following the decision.

"Dear Lord," he had said, a soft quiver in his strong voice. "We are so grateful...*I am so grateful*, you have provided Rachel with a sense of peace and faith in our decision to adopt. Thank you for taking away her pain and providing her with a renewed perspective. I can see the sparkle in her eyes again and I am so grateful you have enabled Holy Spirit's light to illuminate her from within."

His words captured her sentiments so perfectly she was barely able to pronounce *Amen* through her tears of joy and relief.

"I love that you understand," she had told him giving him a hug. "Holy Spirit was always with me. I was the one hiding and not listening. But, it's through God's compassion and His guidance that I've been able to see our circumstance and options differently. I love that you get it. I love that you get me."

"I'm just glad you're back," he had said with a laugh. "What's your schedule look like today?"

"Prayer walk, *Cali's*, and then back here this afternoon to make some calls."

"Agencies?"

"Yeah, I've found a few that sound interesting and then the church provided two that sound good," she said slipping on her sneakers. "I'm heading to the park now. I'll walk you to work."

***

Liberated from the weight of despair her infertility issues had ensnared her with, Rachel refocused her baby obsession to researching adoption. Even though she still maintained a very singular focus, it didn't mess with her emotions in the same way trying to get pregnant did. To a certain degree, adoption was something she could manage and control. Able to put her examination and analysis talents to good work, progression and conclusion seemed determined by her dedication. And, she liked those odds.

Just as Collinsville was coming out of hibernation from a very long, cold winter, Rachel was getting back to her daily prayer walk practice. Since making peace with adoption and letting go of her preconceived ideas about how to start a family, her whole outlook had turned around. No longer angry at her body nor injured at the sight of a pregnant woman, she was filled with hope and excitement for their future child.

Stepping into the park, she inhaled the fresh morning air and basked in the soft sun. A warm, gentle breeze brushed past and she knew He was with her.

"Good morning," she said. "Thank you for helping me through this trial. I am so grateful."

Her heart raced with excitement as she prepared to share her gratitude and many hopes for the future with the Lord. As the breeze kicked up, tossing her hair about, it was almost as if she could sense His excitement as well.

Bowing her head and taking a deep breath, she dove right in, quietly listing off the very many things she was grateful for. Her deepest gratitude was for Cody. She never dreamed she could have a strong and sensitive husband who shared his own intimate relationship with Heavenly Father. She loved how beautifully romantic he was, yet that he was also her best friend; someone she considered both a mentor and confidant. He seemed to truly understand her pain and never once harshly judged or criticized her for her infertility madness, even when she was truly mentally and emotionally unrecognizable.

She equated her walks with divine meditation, mindful only of her conversation with Him. The world around disappeared as she allowed her heart to speak freely reviewing the week's highs and lows, addressing her concerns, and sharing her desires. Just like a regular conversation, occasionally the dialogue would wander. Unlike most areas of her life, she never tried to control it. Through the years, she had discovered this was often His way of directing her thoughts and aiding her in asking the right questions.

Making her way through the park, she could hear her footsteps on the sandy path below and the spring birds chirping above. The auditory awareness was unique, as she typically was not focused on the sounds around her as much as she was listening to her heart. Feeling as though He might be trying to tell her something, she listened closely. In the distance she could hear children playing.

Shouting and laughing, their sweet voices permeated through the park bringing joyful energy to all who could hear. From every blade of grass and woodland creature to every new spring flower and old growth tree, their cheerful sound scattered through the space like glitter seemingly adding a bit of sparkle everywhere it landed. Once again Rachel's heart began to race with anticipation.

"Pray for the children," she heard her heart petition. "Pray for their safety and for their ability to distinguish good from evil."

Yielding to the request, she turned the conversation towards the children of Collinsville and began to pray for their faith. She appealed to the Lord for their earnest desire to do good and live righteously. She prayed that she and the Collinsville community have the ability to provide them with Godly wisdom and guidance, setting a good example and offering them love and support.

Like a mantra, she prayed fervently for their protection and for the protection of those soon coming to Collinsville. She prayed for the safety of Teresa's baby due to arrive any day. And, she prayed for her and Cody's forthcoming child. A soft breeze roused her from the meditation as *God bumps* erupted all over her arms. Raising her head and looking around she found herself just steps from walking into the middle of a baseball game. Startled, she quickly made her way off the field and giggled quietly to herself, relieved she didn't interrupt the game or injure herself.

Taking a seat on a nearby park bench she gathered her thoughts and considered what had just occurred. The deviation from her standard prayer walk threw her for a loop. She was accustomed to the time of devotion leading to spiritual confirmations and guidance from Holy Spirit, but this experience was something new all together. She felt emotionally drained and physically exhausted. Looking at her watch, she was surprised to see it was already noon. She had been on her prayer walk for more than two hours. Quickly gathering her things, she made her way to *Cali's* to check-in with the crew.

***

"Hi, my husband and I are considering adoption. I've heard good things about your agency and was interested in making an appointment to come find out more," Rachel said. She felt like a robot. It was the sixth similar call she'd made in an hour. The introduction was over-rehearsed at this point.

"Wonderful," a man exclaimed on the other end of the phone. With just a single word his enthusiasm jostled Rachel from the redundant nature of the calls and his accent had her curious about his country of origin.

He added, "Adoption is a beautiful thing, my dear."

Her heart leapt, finding truth to his words. "Would it be possible to come by next week?" she asked. "I live a couple hours from the city and am trying to coordinate appointments for Wednesday."

"Yes," he responded. His intonation made it sound as though he could be asking a question.

Unsure, she replied, "Do you have availability this coming Wednesday? Around 11 a.m.?"

"Yes," he repeated.

"Okay," Rachel said, a little weary. She couldn't recall if this agency was one she had found or if the church had recommended them. "So, we're confirmed for Wednesday at 11 a.m.? Do you need my information or anything?"

He began to laugh on the other end. "Eleven on Wednesday is perfect, dear. It'll be very informal. Adoption is very personal, a major life decision. The process is lengthy. Our job is to make sure it's a good match for everyone involved, as the children we represent are vulnerable. The prospective parents can be sometimes, too. You and your husband come by on Wednesday. We'll meet and take it from there. My name is Zane. You will meet me, my wife, possibly my son and his wife…we all run the agency."

"I'm Rachel Brooks," she said, appreciating his human approach. "My husband's name is Cody. We look forward to meeting you all. Thank you."

Hanging up, she looked at the schedule for Wednesday. It was going to be a full day. A trip to the city, six agency meetings at different locations all over Manhattan, and a return to Collinsville was a lot for one day, but she and Cody both had so much going on they needed to pack in as much as they could.

All things aside, *CTB International Adoption Agency* gave Rachel the best feeling over the phone. They were the most personable. The other agencies had been very structured, corporate. Each receptionist had responded to her scripted introduction with a similarly contrived response and had booked an appointment. Like a doctor's office, they offered time slots and an overview of materials required to bring to the meeting. This man, Zane, had invited her to stop by, like a neighbor inviting her by for coffee or a community meet-and-greet. It seemed friendly. It seemed like a good place to start a family.

***

"Okay," Cody said as the New York City skyline came into view. "I've got to ask."

"Ask what?" Rachel inquired with a giggle.

"What're you thinking?" he asked, gently. "You've been quiet, looking out the window, since Poughkeepsie."

"Have I?" she responded, embarrassed. "What a terrible co-pilot — I'm sorry. I was just thinking about my prayer walk the other day. It was different. I mean, I've learned to never assume how or when the Lord will respond, but my walk on Saturday was intense."

"Did you want to talk about it?"

"Yeah," she said with a slight delay. "The only reason I haven't told you already is that I'm still ruminating on what happened. Basically, I was praying about my stuff. Just having a conversation with the Lord about things I'm grateful for. If your ears were burning, it's because I droned on and on about you for quite a while. Then, as I started to pray for the things I am hopeful for, feeling like I need help with, He directed my attention towards the children in the park. I felt an intense

57

need to pray for their safety and protection, for their ability to differentiate between good and evil."

Cody was quiet for a moment. "Sometimes when I pray," he started. "Holy Spirit will help nudge the direction of my prayer or remind me to pray for certain people. Was it like that?"

"Yes," she agreed. "But, a little different. This was similar, but my heart actually appealed to me in a way. Like, it spoke to me. He *requested* that I pray for the children. I know prayer's powerful, but it was as-if my prayers mattered for the children's sake. That was new for me. To think that my prayers were contributing to their well-being and being heard on their behalf. At least I hope so."

Rachel paused and thought for a moment.

"Now, I've been wondering why the prayer was necessary," she added. "I mean, we live in *Collinsville*. It's the most beautifully Christ-focused, family friendly, safe town that I've ever been to. I remember feeling the positive energy when coming to visit my Aunt Cali as a kid. Coming in from New York, everything felt different. It was as if I could see an additional layer of light in the atmosphere. Now, knowing Christ, I believe it's His light. It emanates through all of Collinsville, its people, and places. So, to wonder why the prayer was needed, is a little overwhelming."

"Rach," Cody said, patting her thigh. "Collinsville *is* special. It's filled with Christ's light. Maybe your prayers are just to help ensure it stays that way? You're so in tune with Holy Spirit. It's such a pleasure to witness. I wouldn't let the fact that your prayers have been enlisted to protect our children worry or frighten you."

"Thank you. I know you're right. It just made me uneasy. And, now, here we are driving into New York City to look at adoption agencies, because we're looking to adopt our future child. It just has me wondering what's in store, you know? It has me wondering what the future holds. I just want to make a good decision."

"Deep breath," he said, massaging her shoulder best he could while still driving. "Baby steps."

"Pun intended?" she asked with a laugh.

"Most definitely."

***

Sitting in the waiting room, Rachel reviewed the space. There was a fish tank with beautiful, tropical fish along one wall, a receptionist counter, and a nicely arranged lobby with magazines, adoption information pamphlets, and soft elevator music. It felt like a doctor's appointment. She pulled out her binder and handed Cody a pen and paper.

"What's this?" he asked.

"For notes. I'm going to take pictures with my phone, but I want to have notes about how we feel at each agency. I have a questionnaire I'm working from to get the factual stuff, but if you could just take notes on all the non-cognitive stuff. Like, anything concerning how the office or people make you feel...that would be great."

"Non-cognitive?" he asked, raising an eyebrow. "That's a word I haven't heard since Stanford."

"I'm in my fact-finding and discovery mode," she said, referencing her time as a lawyer. "Just wait until we get to discussing the verdict."

"I look forward to it," he said giving her a supportive smile.

"Mr. and Mrs. Brooks?" a woman called from the office door.

Following her down a hall to a sterile, sunlit room, she motioned for Cody and Rachel to take a seat at a round table.

"Hillary, your adoption advocate, will be in shortly. Can I get either of you a water or coffee?" she asked.

"Coffee would be great," Rachel replied, feeling the effects of their 5 a.m. wake-up call.

They both looked around the room as they waited.

"So, how does this room make you feel?" Cody asked, pen in hand.

"Adequate, I like the windows. I like that it appears we already have someone assigned to help us specifically. But, we'll have to see."

***

"Two down, four to go," Cody said as they left their second appointment for the day. "Do you want to grab a snack?"

Rachel handed him a banana from her bag. "Let's keep going. I was thinking we'd grab lunch at a place I used to love after our 11 o'clock."

Just off Broadway in Chinatown, in the middle of Rachel's old NYU and Tribeca stomping grounds, she thought it would be nice to walk to their next appointment in Little Italy. Cody had never spent much time in the city. Having grown up with grandparents as parents and then going to school in the Bay Area, he didn't have the opportunity. And now, the city typically came to him. His woodworking talents had him on the radar of many wealthy New Yorkers looking for custom pieces to fit their unique city dwellings. So, while Cody was well established with the people, he could count his trips to the city on one hand. Rachel looked forward to giving him a little glimpse of her former life.

As they walked past familiar boutiques and cafes, Rachel shared anecdotes and talked about the things she liked and missed about the city, as well as the things she was grateful to no longer have to deal with.

"We are so spoiled with even the air we breathe in Collinsville," she said. "It's gross, but go home after a long summer day out and about in the city, and when you blow your nose it'll be black with, I don't know what…dirt, grime, soot; probably all of it."

"Really?" he asked.

"Yup," she said. "But, there really is something special

about this place. It's just different. Not special in the same way that Collinsville is special, but special in the sense that no matter what you're into, you can probably find a world-class version of it here. It's a metropolis that's full of beautiful, amazing things, as well as depressing, awful things."

Soon they were at the door to *CTB International Adoption Agency*. Wedged between a Chinese noodle house and a produce market, Rachel's positive first impression from the phone conversation began to wane. With a shrug, she hit the buzzer and heard the door unlock allowing them to enter. Up two flights in a stairwell that echoed their every step, they came to another door. Without a business placard, Rachel hesitantly knocked.

"Hello, Rachel! Hello, Cody!" exclaimed Zane in an exuberant, heavily accented voice as he opened the door. "You, young folk, are quick. I was going to meet you at the door. I know it's not marked. But, you found us nonetheless. Come in, come in."

Zane, a squat and rotund man with a thick head of peppered gray hair, shook each of their hands as he waved them into an inviting room filled with two large leather sofas and a beautiful Persian rug. It felt more like a cozy, warm living room as opposed to any sort of office. It felt like someone's home.

"Sit, sit," he said. "Ursula will be out in just a moment with tea. My son and his wife are just wrapping up some items and they will join us in a little bit as well. I want you to meet them, because not only do they work at *CTB*, but they themselves are adoptive parents. So, I thought their story might be of benefit to you."

"That's very thoughtful," Rachel said, a little taken back by the welcome. Looking over at Cody she could see him scribbling notes which made her smile and relax. "We would love to hear their experience."

Ursula, a sturdy woman with long, silver hair pulled back

in a large, loose bun, entered the room from a hallway carrying a tray. She thoughtfully set down a teapot and tea setting, and plopped down on the couch next to Zane.

"I wasn't sure what sort of tea you would like," she said in an accent similar to her husband's. "The pot has hot water; there are bags in the box." She lifted the lid of an embellished wooden box to display a variety of tea.

"This is perfect," Rachel replied, picking up a cup and saucer to hand to Cody. She flipped through the box and pulled out an herbal mint blend for herself. "I've been drinking coffee since we got up this morning. And, we got up early to get to the city at a decent hour. I am way over caffeinated."

"Yes. I thought it could go either way," she said matter-of-factly. "You were coming from upstate, correct?"

"Uh-huh," Rachel replied. "Collinsville. Have you heard of it?"

"No. But, that doesn't mean anything. We don't leave the city. We are working all of the time," she said unapologetically. "New York is a very tough place to succeed. Very expensive. I worry about my son."

Rachel nodded in agreement while feeling a little sheepish about her abnormal experience living a very lavish life in the city as a young adult. "Yes, it takes a lot of hard work, but also a little luck to be really successful here."

"Tell us a little about yourselves," Zane said, steering the conversation back to the reason they were there. "In particular, we would like to know how you met and how your personal story has led you here today."

Rachel looked at Cody and smiled, silently prompting him to take the question.

"Well, we could probably talk for ages about what led us here today," Cody said. "I can give you the Cliff Notes and then we'd be glad to expound on anything you'd like to hear more about."

Zane waved his hand for him to continue.

"We met in high school. I had a crush on Rachel immediately, but she wasn't too sure about me. I think I was viewed more as competition than anything. Rachel's slightly ambitious and we were both pretty good in school." He looked at Rachel and she smiled.

"I didn't like how suave you were about getting the best grades in class," she said with a laugh. "On the surface it appeared to come too easily for you."

"Little did she know all I did was study. I was always just relieved to not be discovered at the fraud I thought I was!" he exclaimed. "We ended up being good friends. One of the things that really connected us, was our home life. I was being raised by my grandparents and she had just moved in with her aunt. My parents were not involved in my life because of addiction. When she was 14, Rachel's mom died in a terrible accident and her dad wasn't around. We bonded because we were both missing that quintessential parental bond."

Cody paused for a moment and looked at his hands. He glanced at Rachel and took a deep breath. "Anyhow, then we went away to college. I went to Stanford in California and Rachel went off to NYU. Neither of us made an effort to keep in touch. I think we were both sort of embarrassed. Thinking the other didn't feel the same way. In the end, I know we were both saddened by the loss of a close friendship. We finished our undergrad. I began to gain clients with my hobbyist woodwork and across the country Rachel was starting up law school and planning to marry a guy she had met at school. But, stars aligned and nearly 8 years after saying good-bye, we both ended up back in Collinsville, single, and ready to mingle," he said with a crooked smile. "Sorry, I had to lighten the mood...for myself. The story, even told in snip-its, makes me see the Lord's divine plan for me. I tend to get emotional. Like I said, we bonded as kids over our parent-deficit. In my case, I never had a relationship with my parents. They weren't around. In Rachel's case, her dad disappeared when she was young and her mom died when she was 14. My grandparents were amazing. They gave me everything and never made me feel like a burden. I know Rachel's Aunt Cali was the same way. But, we both have a deep understanding of what it's like to feel abandoned. Rachel also has an unfortunately solid grasp on what it's like to lose someone. When we realized we were having difficulty getting pregnant, adoption revealed itself as the right option for us. Looking at our personal stories, it makes sense why our hearts would desire to provide a family and be parents to a child possibly dealing with those same feelings. So, here we are."

Rachel felt tears pushing to get out. She dabbed at the corner of her eyes, hoping to catch any before they escaped.

"Thanks," she said, giving Cody's back a rub. "That was perfect."

She appreciated Zane's question. It was the first agency that had wanted to hear their personal story. Of course, the other agencies had plenty of qualifying questions, but none quite so open-ended or individualized to their specific story.

Zane and Ursula sat and thoughtfully considered Cody's answer.

"Adoption is so personal," Ursula said. "My son and his wife, they've had a different road to deciding to adopt, different reasons. But, in the end, it's about starting a family."

Just then the door opened and a man and woman in their late 20's entered. "Ah, speak of the devil," Zane said, clapping his hands together with excitement. "Rachel, Cody, this is Uri, my son, and his wife, Melinda."

Rachel instantly liked something about Melinda. She was fashionable, a little edgy, had large blue eyes, and blonde hair the same gold tone as her mom and Aunt Cali. Uri was also striking. Unlike Cody, who was handsome in an all-American, charming and welcoming way, Uri was handsome in a dark and brooding way. His face lit up just enough, though, with a smile as they shook hands to put Rachel at ease.

"Sorry we're a little late," he said. "We were checking in with a client preparing to leave for Croatia. In their situation, they are adopting a child from a mother who has decided to not keep her baby. She is due any day, so they want to be on hand."

"Are all of the babies you facilitate adoptions for from Croatia?" Rachel asked.

"We work mainly within Croatia, yes," Uri replied. "My parents and I are Croatian and we have close relationships with a number of religious and secular groups throughout the country that work with us to direct pregnant women in distress to us."

"What are the benefits of adopting from Croatia?" she asked. "Why should we consider adopting a child from so far away when there are children in need here?"

"Again, that is completely personal," Ursula said. "I'm sure Melinda and Uri can share their opinion with you."

Melinda adjusted in her seat as though she wanted to say something, but remained quiet.

"Go on, Uri," Zane prompted. "Tell them your story."

Uri nodded at his father and turned to look at Cody and Rachel. "It's a big decision, adoption."

They both bobbed their heads in agreement wondering where he was going.

"Melinda and I wanted kids as soon as we got married," he started. "I never had any brothers or sisters. And, Mel, well, she grew up with five other siblings. So, we both had a similar mindset for different reasons. Big family. We wanted a big family. We planned to work in the city, pop out as many kids as we could handle and then move to the country where we'd keep having kids and they could run around crazy and free. We'd have a big house full of laughter, stomping, screaming, banging, all of it. We wanted it all."

The story was already making Rachel feel emotional. She

had lost her mind over wanting one child. She couldn't imagine planning for a big family, multiple kids, and not being able to get pregnant.

"Anyhow, we tried for a year on our own to no avail. Mel changed her diet. Nothing. We started looking into IVF; all the while working here. Being very well-versed in the cost of adoption, the price tag for in vitro fertilization was tough to swallow. We were looking at roughly the same expense of $20 to $30K. Plus, when we started to read through all of the side-effects and looked at the less than favorable chance of going through all of it and then still not getting pregnant, adoption started to look pretty good. We don't have an endless bank account. Our ultimate goal was to start a family. You know, have a baby. So, if we were going to spend the money, we wanted to end up with a healthy baby. Adoption ended up being our choice. And, for us, obviously going through *CTB International* made sense. But, even if we didn't work for this agency, we would have looked to adopt a child from Eastern Europe, mostly because we wanted our child to look like they belonged to us. We wanted them to feel like they belonged."

"That's something Cody and I haven't really discussed yet," Rachel said. "But, while I believe we can provide an unconditionally loving, supportive family for any child meant for us, I do worry about the constant questioning if we adopted a child that didn't look like us. I fear that it could exasperate any sense of not belonging if they have to deal with a lifetime of questions. I don't know."

"You do your research. You meet with agencies. And, you think about it; long and hard," Zane said. "Your heart will help you decide."

CHAPTER FOUR
CTB INTERNATIONAL

The decision should have been more difficult. After meeting with all of the agencies in person, she and Cody were struck with utter confusion as to which one would be the best partner in finding their child. Turning to references had proven useless as most of the agencies came highly recommended by people Rachel knew and respected.

Her urgent desire to get the process started overwhelmed her prayer walks and it was difficult to pick up on Holy Spirit's guidance. While she continued to pray for the children of Collinsville, Rachel's overarching theme was a solicitation for an answer. Feeling powerless to stop it, the plea became a demanding mantra by week's end. Feeling left out in the cold, she begrudgingly maintained her prayer walk schedule through the weekend.

On Sunday, in church, as the band reached a fever pitch, Holy Spirit seemed to fill the room as the entire congregation sang out in praise. With every beat of the bass drum, Rachel's heart reverberated in her chest filled with love and excitement for the Lord. In the midst of the impassioned worship, her mind suddenly wandered to her trip to the city. Shuffling through mental images of the day visiting with agencies, she landed on an impression of *CTB International* with Uri and Melinda. The process wasn't the way she typically received revelation. *God bumps* didn't accompany the vision, nor did she feel the reassuring warmth of Holy Spirit's personal attention.

As the band came to a soft, quiet close, Pastor Bishop took to the microphone.

"Dear Lord!" he exclaimed, diving straight into an energetic prayer. "Our God! Our Savior! Our Redeemer! We are filled with joy, overcome with gratitude, that You have brought each one of us here today. We feel Your Spirit among us. Holy Spirit is here! We are inspired by your majesty. We gladly surrender our lives to you in worship and praise. Come dwell in our hearts, teach us, guide us. Challenge us so that we may be more like You! We ask a special blessing for those who are not with us today. Heal those who are sick, comfort those who are hurting, protect those who are away. Father, as we meet now, may we encounter your grace, may we gain insight, and may we be provided with a greater understanding of Your divine ways. Give us answers, Lord. In Your Holy Name, we praise you. Amen."

Throughout the sermon, Rachel's attention faded in and out. Debating whether she had actually received confirmation, she kept glancing over at Cody wondering if he had been given any insight.

"If you feel like God is speaking to you. If you feel like He's telling you to reach out to someone, you already know that He is!" Pastor Bishop exclaimed, breaking her preoccupied thoughts. "Act upon Holy Spirit's promptings and you'll be entrusted with more. Now, let's pray."

After service, as she and Cody made their way out of the worship hall, she grabbed his hand.

"Were you inspired at all?" she questioned, eagerly. "Did anything sway you towards a decision of sorts?"

He smiled. Cody always appreciated her enthusiasm. "No. I'm sorry, Rach. Nothing new on my end. What about you?"

"I think so. I think we should go with *CTB International*."

"Really?" he asked, sounding a bit surprised. "They

weren't one of the agencies recommended by people we know. Why don't you sound confident?"

"Well, I think I received confirmation, but I'm not positive. Maybe we should get a coffee and talk?" she asked, wanting his agreement, his approval.

***

At *Cali's Cafe* they got drinks and found a secluded table outside. Both Cody and Rachel were popular with customers and the team, so it was difficult to hide completely, but they did the best they could. Rachel's head was spinning. She felt so close to finally starting their journey towards parenthood. She desperately wanted to hold their baby — to meet their baby.

"Okay, so let's review," she said clasping her hands around her latte bowl. "Most of the agencies come highly recommended or meet important criteria on my checklist. They all have strong points. Let's look at our wish list."

"I thought we were going to figure out if you'd been given a divinely sanctioned selection?" Cody questioned with a perplexed smile.

"Well, I think I was. I'm just trying to pair that with deductive reasoning. You know, just to be sure."

Cody nodded for her to go on.

"We're flexible on some things. Like we're open to a boy or girl. But the things I think we're firmer on, are that we want an infant, not a toddler or older child. We would like them to appear as though they could physically be our birth child. And, lastly, we don't feel equipped to adopt a child with special needs, right?"

Cody nodded again. "Yes. But, when you break it down like that, it sort of makes us sound like terrible people."

Rachel sighed. "Are we being too particular?" she asked, worried. "Should we put it all in God's hands?"

"I think we should listen to our gut; go with what we're comfortable with to a certain extent, make an educated

69

decision, and then pray about our choice. I believe we need to do most of the legwork. I don't think it's responsible to put it all in God's hands. It's like throwing seeds in the air and hoping they'll land, take root, gain nutrients, sprout, and grow without us doing anything. At least that's my take."

Rachel considered Cody's response. "It makes sense, and maybe that's why we've been so challenged in finding which agency to go with. I know my prayers have mainly been for direction in choosing an agency. Not confirming an agency of choice is correct. So, with that in mind, let's do the math," she said. "We can eliminate four agencies right off the bat."

Cody laughed. "What's your logic?"

"The first agency, working with children and families in the U.S, made it pretty clear that we could end up waiting a very long time if we were specific about things like age and race. The second agency, *From the Heart,* specialized in placing children from Latin America. The fourth agency worked to find homes for orphans 18 months to 14 years old. And, the last agency dealt with areas of Africa. So, those places aren't really a match for our search."

"I see where you're going," he said pausing. "I guess we need to be specific in order to narrow it down."

"That leaves two agencies, both working with children from Eastern Europe; one from Bulgaria and one from Croatia. Do you have a preference?" she asked. "Are you leaning towards one or the other?"

"You know, I've been looking at my notes and reviewing the pictures you took. Honestly, since you've narrowed it down to those two, I do have a preference. I think we both got a really warm feeling from *CTB International.*"

Rachel's heart fluttered. "Okay," she said wrapping her hands around Cody's. "We've made our decision. I think it's time to pray."

***

"Dear Heavenly Father," Rachel prayed, starting in on her

third petition of the day, although it was the first one said in the park. She desperately wanted His stamp of approval on *CTB International*. She had already made an appointment to go in and meet with Uri and Melinda under the guise of getting to know the agency better, but she knew in her heart it was inevitably the beginning. So, she was feeling crunched for time. "Please bless me with patience. I am so eager to get this adoption process started, but I'm looking to you for confirmation."

Suddenly her attention was drawn away. Her ears once again began to pick up on the sounds of children playing. With a smile, she acquiesced to His will and turned the focus of her prayer over to the kids of Collinsville. She knew that God was well aware of her plight and, apparently, her prayers were needed elsewhere.

***

"How was it?" Cody asked loudly from the back deck where he was grilling salmon.

"It was really good," Rachel replied heading out the backdoor to be with him. She gingerly set out placemats and a salad on the table, excited to share the details of her day in the city over dinner.

"I really like Melinda," she said. "Uri's a little dry, or reserved, or something, but Melinda's great. We have so much in common. Well, aside from the fact that she has a big family. But, she also lost her mom when she was young."

"How young?" Cody asked.

"She was 21. She'd just moved to the city from Minnesota. After getting her AA in legal studies, she left home for the first time for a new job as a legal aide. She got the call that her mom had been in a car accident on the Friday of her first week of work."

"That's terrible," Cody said with a heavy breath. "She must've felt so alone. Did she know anyone in the city?"

"Well, that's the bittersweet part of the story. Uri was

71

interning at the law firm. They were the two youngest people there. On Melinda's first day, one of the senior partners told them to go to lunch together and he'd pay for it. So, they went and ended up really hitting it off. By the time Melinda received the call late Friday afternoon, she and Uri had already initiated an early, but sweet, friendship. The instant she found out, he helped her get her flight home and took on some of her workload while she was away. As a side note, I discovered he's now a practicing adoption and immigration attorney, that's his role with *CTB*. I knew he was working for his parents helping to facilitate the adoption process, but he's actually a practicing lawyer. Just on behalf of *CTB* though, which I find a little odd. He could make so much more money if he was a lawyer for hire. I don't know. To each his own, I guess," she said dismissing it with a wave of her hand.

"That's interesting, especially since Zane had complained about money," Cody recalled, setting a piece of salmon on Rachel's plate. "It seems like they would want him to make the most lucrative choice for his family. You're right, though. I'm sure they have their reasons. Anyhow, did you get a better idea about the next steps in the process?"

Fidgeting with her fork, she pushed salad around her plate and cocked her head to the side, considering her response.

"Rachel?" Cody questioned playfully. "What happened?"

"Nothing *happened*," she answered reluctantly. "It's just that after taking so much of their time and getting to know them better, having so much in common with Melinda, and realizing that Uri was an attorney, I sort of, inadvertently, started the adoption process."

"What?" Cody exclaimed in good-humored surprise. "You were so set on waiting for spiritual confirmation. I'm shocked at your fickleness."

Rachel could feel her cheeks turning pink with embarrassment. "I know. Believe me, I know. It just sort of happened. They showed me a picture of their son and then asked if I wanted to read some of the profiles of expectant mothers wanting to place their babies up for adoption, and it just sort of happened."

"But what does that mean?" he asked.

"It's not like I've signed anything. I just made it apparent that we were going to be working with them for our adoption."

"Well, here we go!" he exclaimed, putting his hand in the air for a fist pump. "I'm ready."

Rachel laughed. "I'm glad you're excited," she said. "I just feel like I've jumped the gun."

Reaching across the table to hold her hands, Cody said, "I think there are some things that are okay to decide on your own. You know? You've been mindful of His will throughout this process. We've made a well thought-out decision and placed it before Him. I think silence could be His way of allowing us to move forward with our decision."

Rachel nodded, unconvinced.

"I'll just say that my heart leapt when you said that you had started the adoption process. It felt right. So that has to count for something," he added.

Smiling, she agreed. "That counts for a lot. It actually makes me feel much better."

She suddenly felt a rush of excitement as well. "Woo-hoo!" she hollered, laughing as she imitated Cody's fist pump. "We're coming for you, baby-of-ours!"

***

"You're heading to the city again?" Cody asked a bit taken aback. "What about *Cali's*? What about *Holy Rollers*? Don't you serve lunch today at the shelter in Myford?"

Sitting at the breakfast table, drinking coffee and reading the news on his iPad, he watched as she darted about the kitchen gathering rations for the train ride.

"It's the only day Melinda has available to review profiles with me this week," Rachel said shoving a small box of crackers, a cheese stick, and a lightweight scarf into her bag. "She's going to show me how to access the profiles on their server, so I won't have to go to the city as much; but to be honest, I've enjoyed the time with her. *Cali's* is doing fine, although I do need to refocus and get back in there. There's been a couple of customer complaints recently. *Holy Rollers* has been pushed to Friday. And, I'm playing hooky from volunteering this week."

Cody still looked a bit concerned. "I'm cool with whatever you feel you need to do; you know that," he replied. "And, I'm well aware that you dive headfirst into any passion project. But, I just have this feeling that we need to stay vigilant to our obligations here. I've heard *chatter* about *Cali's* and I have this nagging feeling that *Holy Rollers'* needs to be a priority. With all of the praying He has had you been doing for the kids of Collinsville, it seems like the ideal missionary opportunity. And, well, the shelter's just something that I know has meant a lot to you for a long time…"

He cleared his throat and adjusted in his seat. She knew he didn't want to question her.

"My point is…we can't lose ourselves to this search. It's monumentally important, yes. But, it's super important that we maintain a sense of ourselves through this process."

Rachel knew he was right.

"You've heard chatter about *Cali's*?" she asked following up.

Cody nodded gently and stood. Walking over to her, he wrapped his arms around her and gave her a kiss. "People have just been wondering where you've been."

The last thing Rachel wanted was to tarnish her late aunt's good name. She knew she had been neglecting the business, allowing Maddy and the shift managers to run the show. But, she had honestly thought Maddy, who she had recently promoted to assistant manager, was capable of taking charge in her absence.

"Do you think there's anything going on with Maddy?" Rachel asked.

"I don't know," Cody replied. "I don't think it's a bad idea to check-in with her though; you've been out a lot."

Rachel dipped her shoulders down. "I've been so caught up in working to understand the adoption process, getting to know Melinda, reading profiles of pregnant women, looking at pictures of new babies, and getting to experience the energy of the city again, I've completely neglected my life here," she said suddenly recognizing the point Cody had been delicately trying to relay. "Oh, Cody. I'm sorry."

She paused, giving him a big squeeze back. "Okay, like I said, Melinda is showing me how to access profiles from home today. I'm going to make this one last trip to the city, but I'll call Maddy from the train and schedule a time to meet with her either this evening or tomorrow. You're totally right about *Holy Rollers,* too. I think I may try and do two sessions a week; one for older kids, one for younger...I don't know. I need to think about it. I can't believe you even had to bring it to my attention. I should've thought of it myself."

Taking a deep breath, she wailed, "Ugh! I don't know why I can't maintain a healthy balance in my life when it comes to having a child. What am I going to be like as a *mom*?"

"You're going to be a great mom. Don't even worry about it. We're a team. I'm here to help keep you on track and vice versa. You're not in this alone. That's something to think about, too. I know you want to know the ins and outs of every aspect of adoption; but really, that's why you're working with Melinda and *CTB*. They already know it all, so you can relax and do your part by reviewing profiles...which is hopefully something we can do together, once we have access."

"I love you, Cody Brooks. I love you for being kind, even though, it appears, I have lost all good sense. I love you and I am so grateful to have you as my husband."

"Ditto," he said with a wink.

***

Sitting in *CTB's* cozy reception lounge with Melinda, all Rachel could think about was her meeting with Maddy. She hadn't sounded good on the phone. It wasn't as though she was sick or overwhelmed. It was as if she didn't sound like *herself.* Concerned, Rachel was running through all possible scenarios in her mind as she also tried to pay attention to Melinda's directions.

Working to carefully walk her through the process of accessing the agency's virtual private network and logging in to the client server, Melinda closed her laptop and turned to look at Rachel.

"What's up?" she asked. "I know you didn't catch any of what I just said."

"I'm sorry," Rachel said self-consciously. "I had a bit of a disturbing call on my way here and it seems to be all I can think about."

"Is everything okay?"

"I'm not sure. I called to set-up a time to speak with my assistant manager at *Cali's Closet,* who is also a very good friend, and she just sounded off. I can't place my finger on it; but she was off enough that it was a little upsetting. I'm just eager to go and see her in person."

"Is she on drugs?" Melinda asked matter-of-factly.

"Maddy? No. She'd never," Rachel replied. "I was thinking more along the lines of depression. Collinsville isn't like New York. Drugs and alcohol just aren't really around. So many people in the community, including Maddy, are active, church-attending Christians. Which isn't to say that Christians' don't drink or use drugs; it's just in Collinsville it's very rare to hear about such things. Everyone lives near family and friends and has a really healthy support system. Collinsville is a special place."

"Sounds like Mayberry," Melinda responded with just a twinge of sarcasm.

Rachel started laughing. "You know what? *It is*, in the best possible way. It wouldn't be totally nuts to see Sheriff Andy Taylor sitting down for a cup of cheesecake yogurt or spot Lassie running through the city park. I started going as a kid, because my Aunt Cali lived there. It always had this sparkle to it that the city didn't have. It's hard to describe, really. But, it's like Collinsville has this pure, beautiful light that allows everything and everyone to shine. The air is clean and crisp; even on a hot summer day it's refreshing. And, then, of course, there's the people," Rachel said. "It's like any small town in that there are a few gossipy types and a few curmudgeons, but you still run into them all on Sunday at church putting forth their best effort."

Rachel stopped. "I feel like I'm trying to convert you or something."

Melinda smirked as though she was going to make a smart aleck remark, then suddenly her lower lip began to quiver.

"It's sounds wonderful, Rachel," she said, wiping away a stray tear. "It sounds exactly like what Uri and I were hoping to find once we had a few kids and a substantial savings account from Uri's law practice."

"I didn't mean to upset you. I definitely wasn't trying to rub it in your face. If anything, I was under the impression that you thought it sounded too quaint and silly," Rachel said with hesitation. After taking a moment, she added, "I didn't realize Uri had a practice."

"Errr," Melinda growled with frustration. "He doesn't! He started doing work for his parents and never left. We make okay money, but nothing like what we'd planned on. I feel so trapped. I don't think we'll ever have the ability to get out of the city. It's just paycheck-to-paycheck. We have no safety net."

Rachel was surprised by the admission. Unsure of what to say, she leaned forward and embraced her for a minute while she composed herself.

"I've been through a number of challenges in my life. I know you have too with losing your mom. There's always that moment when you feel completely stuck, like things are never going to change, get better, or feel O.K.; but if you allow yourself the time to take a step back and look from a different perspective, you can typically find a way out of the heartache or struggle that you didn't originally see," Rachel said. "Why don't you, Uri, and little Ivan come out to Collinsville this weekend? We could do an early afternoon barbecue and show you around town."

Melinda rapped her nails on the top of her laptop.

"I'd like that," she said finally. "I need to talk to Uri, but I'm sure he'll be excited at the invitation. I think he's been feeling stuck as well. Maybe going to Collinsville, a place we'd imagined for our family so long ago will help rekindle our motivation to make a change."

"It definitely couldn't hurt. I'll plan to see you all on Saturday, unless I hear otherwise," Rachel said standing to leave. "I've got to head out to go meet with Maddy, but stay positive. It will all work out."

"Thank you," Melinda said giving Rachel a hug. "I'll email you information on how to connect to our VPN and access the server. If you have any issues, we can talk about it on Saturday."

***

Sitting at the back desk across from Maddy, Rachel felt as though her life had been lived in fragments over the past month; at least that was all she could remember. Snippets of New York, pieces of prayer walks in the park, short conversations with Cody. She couldn't recall when she had seen Maddy beyond Teresa's baby shower, which was weeks ago. And, if she was being honest with herself, she really hadn't seen her aside from that party.

Maddy sat fidgeting with the rings in the management binder as Rachel worked up the courage to speak with her friend like a boss.

"I'm sorry I haven't been around this month," Rachel started. "Cody and I have decided to adopt and I've been making trips to the city to meet with an agency. I've been totally caught up in the process and neglecting my role here."

"That's so exciting," Maddy said without the enthusiasm the words suggested. "Congratulations."

"Thanks, it could take some time, but we're excited," Rachel replied. "Anyhow, I wanted to meet and check-in; hear how things are going."

"Things are same old, same old," Maddy said with a sigh. "Not much ever changes here in Collinsville."

"There've been a few complaints," Rachel said. "Which is probably more alarming than it needs to be. I'm sure it's common for businesses like ours, but I know Cali took a lot of pride in never once having a complaint. It's something that I've sought to maintain since taking over; and, until recently, we had been successful. There have been at least three that I know about in the past month. Do you know anything about those?"

"Sure," Maddy said without regret. "They weren't *real* complaints, Rach. All three were from old people at the cafe who were just grumpy. One thought the music playing was too loud. One thought we should serve danishes past 11 a.m., and the last one was angry that we ran out of almond syrup."

Rachel cleared her throat and paused to think about her response.

"Were you the manager on duty for all three situations?" Rachel asked.

"Yes. And, I spoke with all three of them. They all happened to be people from out of town…really unpleasant. I think they were from the city. Not that all people from the city are unpleasant," she added giving Rachel an apologetic smile. "They just weren't as forgiving as people from Collinsville. I always tried to rectify the situation."

"I'm sure you did," Rachel said sympathetically. "Okay, so enough about work…why don't you tell me how you're doing? You seem a little down. You just don't seem like yourself."

Maddy tilted her head and looked at Rachel with a wounded, almost angry expression.

"I'm fine," she said quietly. "I mean, I'm fine if you don't count the fact that *Cali's* is my entire life. I don't do anything besides work here and try to make sure things are running smoothly. I was here on Monday from 6 a.m. until 6 p.m. opening the cafe, placing the week's orders, reviewing the numbers from the weekend, putting up the new display window for the boutique, and just working with the team. Everyone is bending over backwards to make sure this place maintains business as usual while you work through whatever it is you're dealing with."

Rachel felt herself recoil at the assertion. Looking at Maddy, she tried to think of an excuse, a way to justify her absence and apparent disregard for *Cali's*. Suddenly she could hear her heart appeal for her not to engage in a back and forth. Both of their feelings were sincere and frayed; Rachel needed to do what she could to soothe Maddy's.

"Thank you, Maddy," Rachel said touching her friend's hand. "Thank you for being honest with me. You're right. I haven't been around enough. I'm sorry that you've needed to pick up the slack. I feel terrible that everyone feels so overworked."

Maddy looked relieved. Rachel thought she looked physically lighter. It was as though a weight had been lifted from her shoulders.

"I was nervous to say anything. But, I'm burned out; so, it was bound to come out one way or another," Maddy confirmed with a lighthearted laugh.

Rachel gave her a big hug. She was grateful she had avoided a potentially difficult and confrontational conversation. She was eager to get back to work at *Cali's* and show her staff how much she cared.

"What do you think would be a nice thing to do for the team?" Rachel asked. "I'd like to do something to show how much I appreciate their hard work; but also help them relax a bit. I feel terrible that everyone's felt so overworked. The dedication is amazing; but I never expected everyone to work 12-hour days or lose sleep over feeling so responsible for *Cali's*. I wish you would've called and let me know sooner."

"I didn't want to bother you," she said. Then, shifting in her seat a bit, added, "I don't know if any sort of group activity is a good idea. Everyone's a bit on edge with each other."

"What?" Rachel asked shocked. "But, we have such a nice team. What's happened over the past month, Maddy? I don't understand."

Maddy shrugged her shoulders. "I don't know. To be honest, I've noticed it everywhere in Collinsville. I'm not sure if it's an invasion of people from the city, no offense, or just a dark cloud hanging over town; but I'm just feeling terribly depressed about it. I haven't had to field so much anger in my entire life. It's coming from customers, employees...I even had Mr. Watson's dog bark at me yesterday. You're the first person who's been kind and patient, which is amazing because I didn't start off our conversation very well. It's awful. The bad attitude is like a virus. I totally had it, until you helped me snap out of it."

Rachel felt a cool breeze blow in from the open back door. Looking down her arms were covered in *God bumps,* but they felt different this time. She wondered if they might actually be goosebumps. She looked her friend in the eyes and was so happy to see the shimmer of light she was accustomed to, but she was troubled by her claim. Could Collinsville really be full of grumpy people, she wondered? Peering outside, she could see a beautiful blue sky melting into the earthy dark tones of evening; but the sparkle was missing.

Her heart sank. Thinking better of it, she decided it was because it was dusk, and the power of suggestion.

"We'll have a team meeting Monday night. We'll close early and do dinner and stuff at my place, maybe read something inspirational…get everyone feeling open and kindhearted," Rachel said. "I'm sorry you've been dealing with this alone, Maddy."

***

"How was the drive?" Cody asked taking an armful of bags from Melinda.

"Good, good," Uri replied, wrestling to keep their 16-month-old son, Ivan, in his arms. "It was only about two hours. Not bad at all. I must ask, though, what in the world is *cheesecake yogurt?*"

Rachel started laughing.

"Welcome to Collinsville," she said. "*Watson's* is on our itinerary today, so you'll get to experience cheesecake yogurt firsthand."

He smiled, but still looked confused.

"It was a beautiful drive," Melinda said. "That tunnel of trees was so amazing. I think I frightened Ivan with my squeals of excitement…he's used to his mom being a bit more composed."

"That's been one of my favorite things about Collinsville for as long as I can remember. This is the best time of year to see it, although autumn is pretty good too," Rachel added. "Let's get you guys situated and get going! We have so much we want to show you before you have to head home; there's *Watson's*, the park, *Cali's*, and so much more.

***

"Do you think they liked it?" Rachel asked Cody as they got ready for bed.

"I do," he said enthusiastically. "I thought Uri's eyes were going to bug out of his head when he took his first bite of cheesecake yogurt. And they both looked as if they were going to hold hands and skip off into the sunset walking through the park. Little Ivan seemed pretty happy too, he definitely liked the ducks. I would say he was also quite a fan of the vanilla steamer from *Cali's*. The country seemed to suit them."

"Did you see Melinda's face light up when I pointed out the vacant storefront on Main Street?" Rachel remarked. "Although, I don't think any of them were feeling Collinsville Community Church. They seemed bewildered as to why we would take them there."

"Well, I get the impression God, and especially church, isn't something that plays a very prominent role in their life. Collinsville Community is the cornerstone of this town. It would've been misleading to not expose them to that. I wouldn't worry about it," Cody said.

"Oh, I agree," Rachel said taking a seat on the bed and checking her phone. "I just noticed the high-spirited mood shifted when we pulled up. Ah, her ears must have been burning. Melinda just texted."

"What'd she say?"

Rachel grabbed Cody's arm with excitement. "She says, 'Thanks for a perfect day. Just heard back from the landlord. Space still available. VERY affordable. Talk soon!,'" Rachel read. "Can you believe it? She already contacted Watson about the space for rent. Looks like we could have new neighbors soon."

CHAPTER FIVE
SPIRITUAL VULNERABILITY

Rachel could think of few things more delicious than the scent of rich, cold brew coffee poured over ice on a warm summer morning. With the sunlight streaming into the cafe's large windows, Frank Sinatra on the stereo, and the first morning rush just settling down, she grabbed her icy pick-me-up and headed to the back room to check inventory and start on payroll.

"Hello there, neighbor!" Melinda said, peeking her head in the backdoor.

Rachel hurried over to give her a big hug.

"How's the space? Have you been able to get settled in? Are Zane and Ursula happy?" Rachel asked.

Melinda giggled.

"Curious much?" she asked with a big smile. "Yes, the whole family's really excited. The office is beautiful. And, thanks to you and Cody, we're already very well situated. Everyone has been so welcoming and generous. From the point we arrived with the moving van yesterday through this morning, all of our neighbors have stopped by to say hello and introduce themselves. We've received gifts of cookies, a beautiful plant, welcome cards, a cute little Collinsville tee for Ivan, and a huge platter of homemade frozen lasagna from Doris, who actually reminds me a lot of my mom."

"I'm so glad," Rachel said. "I really hope you're able to

find the life you planned on in Collinsville. Regardless, I know I'm happy you're here."

"It sure feels promising," she said in awe. "What luck to have connected with you! Now, we have a home with land, an office within walking distance that we can afford, great friends, and a charming community. I never would've pictured this possible a couple of months ago. Like I said we felt completely trapped. Thank you, Rachel. Thank you to both you and Cody. You have really changed our lives."

She gave Rachel a big hug and then stiffened recalling something.

"Oh, I wanted to let you know, I still haven't heard back about the woman you were interested in from the directory. This sometimes happens. It's never clear why. I imagine once in a while the women change their minds or something. But, I think it would be good for you and Cody to select a handful of women that sound interesting, as opposed to getting your hearts set on one and getting disappointing news; or in this case, no news at all. Once we have a few to inquire about we'll have a better chance of finding the birthmother of your future baby."

"Thank you. I've been dying to ask, but with your move I didn't want to add any stress. I appreciate you keeping on top of it."

"Of course!" she exclaimed. "Remember, I know what you're going through. I've been there. I know it's hard. Exciting, but hard."

Rachel nodded and offered a grin she hoped didn't look too forced.

"Let me know if you need anything," she offered. "I'll be here all day."

"Thanks, Rach. Do you want to pop by the office this afternoon for a little bit? I'll connect with our people in Croatia again and see if we can't get an answer on the woman you're interested in. In the meantime, we can look at a few more profiles?"

"I would love if you'd try one more time," Rachel said. "I really liked what she said in her profile. I'll see if I'm able to sneak away around 2 p.m. for a bit."

***

Stepping into the park, Rachel felt a soft chill wash over her. It had only been a couple of days since her last prayer walk; but it was as if she had just put her hand on one of the electric toys at the Oktoberfest Carnival. Her entire being was awakened and charged. She didn't understand what filled her time so completely that she ever considered skipping one of her precious meditations with Holy Spirit. The opportunity to walk with Him offered such a sense of pure joy, and relief, she vowed to get back to her daily practice again.

"Dear Heavenly Father," she whispered. "I need your help."

Clenching her hands together at her heart as she meandered down the familiar path, she self-consciously scanned her surroundings. Then feeling silly for worrying about what anyone else thought, she squeezed her eyes closed and continued.

"I need your guidance, Dear Lord. I need patience. But, I also need assurance and comfort. I feel like something isn't right. I dreamt there weren't any babies last night. It was like the agency was a bakery that had just sold the last cinnamon roll. Cody and I just stood at the door staring at the *"Closed"* sign, crying. Please bless me with guidance..."

"Rachel?" a sweet, familiar voice came from behind.

Rachel spun around to find Susan Bishop, the pastor's wife of Collinsville Community Church. Not only did she brighten a room with her spirit, with her shiny blonde hair, giant pearly grin, and trendy outfits, she seemed to be the physical embodiment of sunshine. Rachel had loved her from the first moment she saw her at the Collinsville bible camp, known as *Cx3*. After accepting Christ into her heart, Rachel was introduced to prayer walks as a way to maintain her relationship with Holy Spirit by her Aunt Cali and Susan Bishop; and she was eternally grateful.

"Am I interrupting you?" Susan asked offering her familiar, beaming grin.

"No," Rachel said with a sigh of relief. "I was just on my prayer walk."

"Oh, Rachel!" Susan exclaimed. "That's wonderful. I'll let you get back to it. So happy to see you've stuck with the practice. We can catch up another time."

Susan gave Rachel a swift squeeze and turned to leave.

"Wait, no. You're *really not* interrupting," Rachel replied taking her by the arm. "I think you might be the answer to my prayer. Do you have a few minutes?"

"Of course!"

Rachel felt her fear melt away as Susan linked elbows with her. They walked the park's familiar paths together as Rachel told her all about their decision to adopt. She described how they went about selecting *CTB International*, and she explained her concerns about not waiting for a true spiritual confirmation.

"I've made friends with Melinda," Rachel said. "She's really sweet and we've got quite a bit in common; but there's something not quite right. It's been more than a month and, while they've been able to manage an entire *move* to Collinsville, they haven't been able to connect us with any of the prospective birthmothers we've expressed interest in. I'm beginning to feel like we're getting the runaround. I don't know what to do. Especially now that they're here and Melinda and I are close, it feels so awkward. Plus, I'm questioning if I can trust *my* judgment on anything, it seems all of my initial thoughts and opinions are wrong. I feel so far away from Holy Spirit right now. I haven't heard from Him in so long."

Susan stopped walking and wrapped her hands around

Rachel's.

"Sweetie, He speaks to you in His own way and in His own time. You can't demand answers, you can't give Him ultimatums, and you can't get upset when He doesn't respond in a way that you want or anticipate. Who knows, He may be working through you in other ways right now. You might be the answer to someone else's prayers, which can be an amazing blessing in and of itself," she said in such a way that felt like a sweet, gentle reminder, not high-handed. "He loves you, girl. He wants to give you everything you desire, but He always knows what you *need*. It's important to keep in mind that He hears you. It's not as if your prayers are falling on deaf ears. He's with you always. You know that. When we feel as though there is a divider between Holy Spirit and us, it's us, not Him. We build the pavilion over our heads, not the other way around."

Susan pointed toward the park's beautiful, white gazebo off in the distance as an example. Rachel had always found its ornate bracing and wooden posts covered in soft pink climbing roses incredibly charming.

"I heard a very wise man once say, 'The ceiling that seems to obstruct His divine love doesn't cover God, but occasionally covers us. God is never hidden; but we sometimes are.'"

Susan took Rachel's hand and guided her towards the gazebo to sit down. As they sat together on the bench, a soft, warm breeze swirled past bringing with it the elusive, subtle scent of the roses. Susan clasped her hands to her mouth with excitement.

"Do you feel that?" she asked. "He's with us now, sweetie."

"He is, isn't he," Rachel agreed. "I'd almost forgotten how He spoke to me."

"Let's pray together?" Susan asked eagerly.

Nodding her head, Rachel bowed her head and delicately

slipped her fingers into Susan's outstretched hands.

"Dear Lord, our dear and gracious Heavenly Father, thank you so much for bringing Rachel and I together this beautiful day. Thank you for knowing how much we needed to hear from one another. We are blessed by this friendship rooted in our faith in you. Oh God, we love you, and I ask a special blessing over Rachel. Please Lord, give her discernment. Give her the ability to know good from evil. Bless her with unwavering faith and let her heart have peace. Watch over and guide her and Cody in their adoption process. And please get this girl a baby!" Susan exclaimed squeezing Rachel's hands. "Lord, we love and honor you. In your holy name we praise you, Amen."

Rachel was struck by how closely Susan's prayer for her echoed her own prayer for the children of Collinsville. She felt a warmth wash over her. Looking down at her arms she was ecstatic to find *God bumps*. She gave Susan a big hug.

"Thank you."

Susan smiled at her and said, "He loves you. He yearns to talk with you, to have a personal relationship with you, always. Not just when you need answers."

"I needed this reminder," Rachel said. "I've just never wanted anything as much as I want this family. It has totally consumed me. It's made it really difficult for me to quiet my mind, and my heart. I feel like I've got a continuous flow of white noise blasting through my body, drowning out anything but my own desire for a baby. I thought it went away when we decided to adopt, but apparently not."

"You're human after all!" Susan said with a burst of laughter. "I'd question it if you felt any other way."

They stood to say good-bye to one another.

"I want to meet Melinda, and Uri, if possible. Shoot, I'd love to meet the *whole family*. Any chance you'd be able to get them to come to church on Sunday?" she asked.

Rachel considered the question for a moment.

"I don't know. I've brought up God and religion only a couple of times around them and every time I've been met with obvious disinterest. But, I've never outright invited them to church. I'll try. If not, I'm sure I could get them to the house for a potluck. It's that time of year again. It's June 21st...officially summer, we should have everyone over Sunday evening."

"It's a date," Susan said with a wink. "All right, my dear, carry on with your prayer walk. I love you, girl. See you soon."

Rachel gave her a big hug good-bye and closed her eyes.

"Thank you, Lord. I know you hear me. Thank you for knowing who I should talk to and blessing me with Susan. I feel inspired and spiritually uplifted. Talking to her was exactly what I needed and I am so grateful. Thank you, again. In your name, Amen."

***

Handing Cody a mug of hot chocolate, Rachel took a seat with him on the porch swing. Resting her head on his shoulder, she looked out at the stars and recalled the first time she realized what a difference there was between the nighttime sky in New York City and Collinsville. *Who would've thought so many stars were hiding in plain view*, she thought; and then recalled Susan's quote about the covering that seems to obstruct God's divine love doesn't cover Him, but occasionally covers us.

"Maybe I'm just blinded by a sort of light pollution," Rachel said.

"What?" Cody asked with a chuckle. "I feel like I missed the lead-up to that."

"Oh, sorry," she said. "I was just thinking about when I was a kid. I'd never seen a star until I got to Collinsville. Literally. Well, I'd obviously seen the sun; but the only thing beyond the moon, bright enough in the night sky to shine through all of the city lights was Venus, which looked like a star, but it wasn't. The first time I was sitting in Aunt Cali's backyard and the sun began to fall, it was absolutely awe-inspiring. It still is."

"What does that have to do with you being currently blinded by light pollution?"

"Well, you know, I've had a tough time finding that divine light lately, that special sparkle. I was trying to draw a parallel, think about what in my life is possibly acting in the same way the city lights did, blocking out the stars."

"Huh," he said. "I like that. I'm sure we all have a little 'light pollution' now and again. What was your solution as a kid? In order to see the stars, what'd you do?"

"I planned a trip to go see Aunt Cali," Rachel said with a giggle.

"Maybe you need to plan a trip to go see God," Cody replied matter-of-factly. "I mean, not literally; but kind of. Why not take a week and be just completely and utterly focused on Him?"

"Like a God retreat?"

"Yeah. It won't be perfect, since you'll still have to go to work and stuff; but you could just tune out from the world and tune into everything that helps you see Him more clearly. Read scripture at every chance you get, listen to Christ-centered music, watch inspirational shows. You know? Surround yourself with things that'll turn down the light pollution and pump up the stars."

"Why didn't I think of it before?" Rachel asked. "I had the best conversation with Susan Bishop today at the park. It left me feeling totally spiritually jazzed, but at the same time made me realize how long it'd been. I want to build upon that...keep it going."

"I support that completely," Cody said giving her a kiss.

***

"Hey there, chickadee," Melinda said as she poked her head in *Cali's* back door. "You busy?"

Rachel set down her order form and turned down the Christian music she was listening to. Walking over to greet her friend, she got the impression something was wrong.

"Hey, there," she said, grabbing her a chair. "How are things?"

"Oh, I don't know," Melinda said with hesitation. "I think it's just the stress from the move, but…"

Not wanting to pry, Rachel sat quietly as she waited for her to continue.

Getting distracted, Melinda looked around the backroom and honed in on the music playing softly.

"What're you listening to?" she asked with a hint of disdain.

Rachel picked up her phone. "I'm not sure who the artist is," Rachel replied, ignoring Melinda's sneer. "But, it's a song on one of Pandora's Christian stations."

"I know this song. We used to sing this song at church," Melinda replied with a distant look in her eyes. "I haven't heard it since I was probably 16. That seems like another person, it was so long ago."

Realizing she didn't have disdain for the song, but the feelings it was cultivating, Rachel pressed pause and set her phone down.

"Was that before your mom died," she asked knowingly.

"Uh-huh," Melinda mumbled. "She was one of those people who made you want to be better, because she was so amazing. I think all of us sort of hated going to church, even my dad; but it was important to her, so the whole family rallied every Sunday."

"*God,* those are bittersweet memories," she continued with a sad laugh. Rachel cringed at the way she used the Lord's name. "It was such an innocent, joyful time. Everyone was still at home. No one had left for school or gotten married. My mom was adamant that Sunday's be kept for church and family. There was no running to the store, or team

92

SPIRITUAL VULNERABILITY

sports, or friend's birthday parties. It was just thc lot of us
scarfing down her delicious pancakes and bacon, tossing on
church clothes, and heading out the door to make the 10 a.m.
service. My siblings and I would sit and play games through
the whole thing. But, occasionally, I would catch a bit of a
song or the sermon and it would sort of make me think or
cause my heart to flutter a bit. I always liked that hymn..."

Melinda waived her hands in the air dismissing the
memories, "Anyhow, like I said that was a lifetime ago. Me at
church," she said with a giggle. "Now, there are real world
things to worry about, right? Like my in-laws."

Rachel sat quietly for a moment. She was well into the
fourth day of her *spiritual detox* (as she had lovingly started to
refer to it) and there was something very caustic about
Melinda's mood. It was odd how much she loved the notion
of Collinsville, but not what the town was built on. The
church was everything to nearly everyone in Collinsville, and
even those who didn't attend or didn't consider themselves
religious, still had an inherent respect. On one hand Rachel
wanted to preach to her about her beliefs and tell her all about
what God had done in her life. On the other hand, however,
she felt an immense compassion for Melinda and wanted to
help her, in turn *showing* her all about her beliefs. A little
voice in her heart told her not to worry, she'd get plenty of
time to share her testimony.

Silently she thanked Holy Spirit for His divine direction
and took Melinda's hands in hers.

"What's going on with the in-laws?" she asked.

"Oh," she cried. "They've always been a little
challenging. Ursula in particular. But, we've never shared a
home together. I don't know what I was thinking! It's such a
beautiful house. It's everything Uri and I ever wanted, but the
circumstances are so different from what I'd envisioned. We
moved here so quickly. Uri and I never even had a real heart-
to-heart, or any sort of formal discussion, about them moving

with us. Zane and Ursula asked if they could join and when we realized it would enable us to bypass a starter home and go straight to the dream home, we went for it."

Rachel could feel her pain. She understood where she was coming from far better than she could possibly tell her.

"I'm so sorry to hear that," she started. "I'm actually completely unsure of what to say, simply because I am dealing with something similar right now and haven't quite figured out what the solution is. While it's not difficult in-laws, I jumped into something a little too quickly and am not sure it was the right decision."

"Really? We're both smart, why be so hasty?" Melinda asked, seemingly of herself more than Rachel. "And, to top it off, there's something really bizarre going on with the agency. I've always felt on a fairly need-to-know basis, but now that we're all living and working together 24-7, I feel even more in the dark when it comes to the business. Uri has been working nonstop, but then, as you've witnessed, there just isn't a lot of prospective birthmothers. I don't know…it's just annoying."

A visceral heat ran up Rachel's spine and caused her cheeks to burn with a subtle anger. It wasn't directed at Melinda, she didn't think. It was more directed at the agency and receiving confirmation that something was amiss.

"You really think something's going on?" Rachel asked. "Do you think there's just a lack of candidates right now? Is there more demand than, for lack of a better term, supply? Or do you think there's something specifically off with *CTB*?"

"I don't know. I guess that's what I'm trying to figure out. I'll let you know when I do," she said regretfully. "Thank you for listening. It's made me feel better just getting it off my chest. It's sort of consoling to know, I'm not the only one dealing with buyer's remorse."

Rachel offered a weak smile. As Melinda stood to leave, she felt impressed to say just a bit more.

"You know," she started wearily. "When I have a big decision to make, I pray for spiritual confirmation. It may sound woo-woo to you, but normally I'll receive a feeling similar to the heart flutter you mentioned you used to feel sometimes in church."

Melinda looked unfazed as she continued for the backdoor. "Oh, that's not woo-woo. I believe it completely. I'm just way too far-gone for God to ever listen to me. Why didn't you pray for confirmation this time?"

Stunned by Melinda's response, Rachel flipped through her mind to find an appropriate response to the detrimental misconception Melinda had about God's love and accessibility.

"Oh my *God*," Melinda exclaimed, cutting off Rachel's attempt and assailing her sensitive nature again. "I'm totally late for an appointment. Let's catch up later. Thank you again for listening."

Feeling as though she'd just been struck by a tornado, Rachel sunk down in her seat and pressed play on her music. As the gentle piano filled the quiet backroom, she felt an assemblage of her former spiritual tranquility return. Looking at her order form, she couldn't get Melinda's statement out of her mind. It was terrible that, for whatever reason, she believed she was too far from God for Him to care. Rachel felt an overwhelming sense of compassion for her friend and wanted to, at the very least, help her to understand she was misguided in believing such a thing. Even more, Rachel hoped this was maybe an opening to invite her to attend Collinsville Community Church.

At 5:30 p.m., Rachel bid *Cali's* closing team farewell and headed out for the evening. Sipping on an iced tea, she walked quickly, excited to see Cody. Still pursuing her spiritual detox, she put in her earbuds and played a favorite sermon from a series she had downloaded about living a Christ-centered life. When the crosswalk turned green, she stepped forward to cross the street home. Suddenly a car speedily whizzed past, honking loudly, almost as if they were reproaching her for being in their way. Rachel jumped back with shock and fear, her heart racing.

"Who was that?" she questioned out loud. No one in Collinsville drove so aggressively, and Rachel's heart sank to think it was possibly a tourist from the city. "What's happening to our sweet little hamlet?"

Cautiously and quickly making her way across, she looked around to see if anyone else had seen her near mishap. Disappointed to not find any spectators to commiserate with, she spotted Melinda and Uri in the distance walking home. Wanting to turn a blind eye and rush home to Cody's arms, Rachel decided to go against her initial instinct and started in their direction.

"Hey, Rach," Melinda shouted. "Going home for the night?"

"Yep, you guys too?"

"Sort of. We're meeting with another family this evening. We're heading home for dinner, then back to the office."

Every time Melinda mentioned another family it made Rachel feel as though they were cheating on her and Cody's application process. She knew it was silly, and didn't think that was really how it worked, but she wondered if the other families were making more progress; and that idea made her envious.

"Well, I wanted to ask you earlier, but didn't get the chance. I was wondering if you guys were interested in attending Collinsville Community Church on Sunday," Rachel blurted out, fearful she'd never get it out unless she just hurled the words out of her mouth. "It's sort of *the* thing to do in Collinsville on Sundays."

"*The* thing, huh?" Uri questioned with a chuckle.

"I actually think we have an appointment already scheduled for Sunday morning in the city," Melinda responded looking uncharacteristically tense. "Thanks, though, for the invitation."

"Okay, sure," Rachel replied feeling as though she had just asked them to eat worms. "If you make it back in time, we're having a big potluck at our place Sunday evening. Almost everyone in town comes. It'd be a great opportunity to get to know people."

"Are there other families with little ones?" Melinda asked.

Rachel found it an odd and irritating question. She thought, *if they would just get to work and find me a baby, I'd be a family with a little one*. Reminding herself that wasn't a very Christ-like way of looking at the situation, she took a little breath.

"Of course. Teresa and her girls will be there. She's awesome. I would love for you to meet her. Occasionally a family from Myford comes and they have a 5-year-old and an 18-month-old. I'm trying to remember if there are other one's close to Ivan's age. There are lots of families."

"I'd love to start connecting with some other moms," Melinda said looking at Uri. "Can we try to get back in time for the pot luck?"

"Sure," he said. "We can bring a couple of pizzas."

"Oh, jeez," Melinda said smacking his shoulder playfully. "You're so full of it."

Rachel smiled, feeling as though she'd missed the joke. "Don't worry about bringing anything. Just come and have fun. We've got the menu covered and then some."

"Thanks, Rach. By the way, we are working on connecting with your selected birthmothers to get more information. We should have something for you next week."

Offering a weak smile, Rachel nodded and turned to head home. "See you all Sunday."

***

Cleaning up after the morning rush, enjoying a sweet conversation with her co-workers about their plans after high school graduation, Rachel felt her heart swell with love for the young people surrounding her. *These are my kids right now*, she thought. Understanding she wielded influence with them, she thoughtfully worked to make each of them feel special in their choices. Although, it was hard to not be biased and reminisce about her time at NYU with Carissa, who was excited about her recent acceptance.

When the chime of the front door rang, they all paused and looked up to greet the arriving customer.

"Hi, Melinda," they all sang in unison.

She smiled brightly at everyone and waived gingerly like a beauty queen sitting on a float. It made Rachel feel like she may have caught a glimpse of the girl Melinda was back in Minnesota.

"Hey, do you have time to chat?" she asked approaching the cafe counter.

"Sure," Rachel replied. "Let me put my apron in back and I'll meet you at a table out front. Do you want anything?"

"No, thanks," she said softly.

Taking a seat at her and Cody's regular secluded spot, Rachel sat slowly wondering what Melinda was going to talk about now.

"I'm sorry about the other day," she started.

Confused, Rachel wasn't sure what she was referring to. "Sorry about what?"

"I'm sorry I wasn't more receptive when you invited us to church on Sunday. To be honest, I wouldn't mind going. But, Uri…he sort of hates church…well, religion. How do I put this? He's a very proud atheist."

"Don't even worry about it. I wasn't offended by the rejection," Rachel said brushing it off. "I'm glad you guys'll try to make the potluck."

"Oh, I plan to be there. I really want to be there," Melinda replied picking up a straw wrapper from the table and winding it around her fingers nervously.

"There's no pressure," Rachel said trying to reassure her. "This is the first of many Sunday summer potlucks. We'll have them well into the beginning of September. So, please don't feel stressed about making it."

"Oh," she sighed. "That's not stressing me out. It's just the in-law situation again. They're so odd. It's hard. There's not only a cultural and generational divide, but there's also a life perspective divide. I think it's because they lived through war. We're really butting heads on almost everything. It's a disaster."

"That's awful," Rachel said. "I'm so sorry to hear. That's a lot of differences. And a war? That's intense and I'm sure it's changed the way they look at everything. What war?"

"The Croatian War of Independence in the early 90's," Melinda said. "It was hard on them. It's actually when the agency started because there were so many orphaned kids. But, a lot of things have changed since then. And, they aren't willing to change with the times…they aren't willing to change with anything."

"I'm sorry. It's got to be extra hard not getting any sort of a break. I'm sure it was much easier to let stuff go when you were able to leave it at the office."

"I knew you'd get it," Melinda responded sounding relieved. "I can't talk to Uri about it. Even though he's annoyed by some of the same stuff, he has so much love, respect, and sympathy for them, he defends them anytime I try to vent."

"Yeah, that's a sticky place to be. You don't want him to feel like he has to pick sides," Rachel said with a nod. "Is there a way to make them living with you a positive thing? Like, what about setting aside two nights a week as date nights? Have Ursula and Zane watch Ivan while you and Uri get out for a bit on your own? I mean, you have built-in babysitters. Or what about doing something fun, like swapping dinner nights. Where Ursula and Zane are responsible a few nights a week, and then you and Uri get a couple nights a week."

"It sounds so easy when there aren't personalities involved," Melinda replied. "You're right, though. I really need to make the best of it. My bad attitude isn't helping anything. Ursula's great with Ivan. She loves him so much. She's always happy to watch him. I totally take for granted that she does normally cook for all of us. While I don't always love her food; I should be more grateful for the effort she puts into it."

Then, turning her head and staring off into the cafe, Melinda added quietly, "But, I don't know…I came down early this morning because I couldn't sleep and I was in desperate need of a cup of coffee. When I got to the kitchen door, I could hear them talking."

"Who, Ursula and Zane?" Rachel asked.

"Yes. They were in the kitchen. Zane was sitting, reading the morning paper, and Ursula was making him breakfast. He had just read some statistic in the *Collinsville Courier* about how the town consisted of the greatest number of townies, natives to the city, than any other town in the state of New York. It was a very high number, establishing that there just aren't a lot people moving in or out. Anyhow, Zane told Ursula the statistic, explained what it meant, and then added, 'The perfect place to hide, no?,' Ursula put her finger to her lips, as if she were motioning for him to be quiet and that was it."

"What?" Rachel asked a little confused. "I'm not sure I follow."

"Well, of course, because it's weird," Melinda said with a look of distaste. "Why would he say that? Even if it's a joke, why would he be thinking about something like hiding out? From whom? It's the strangest thing to say and totally gave me the willies."

"Is it possible he knew you were listening?" Rachel

questioned. "I only ask because whenever I've seen the two of them alone, they tend to speak Croatian to each other. Why would they say it in English?"

"*God,*" Melinda replied, causing Rachel to cringe. "I didn't think of that. I really needed coffee, so it would've been all too easy to pull my leg. Do you really think they were messing with me?"

"It seems out of character from the interaction I've had with them. But, then again, our relationship has been strictly business," Rachel said. "Is it totally out of the question to just ask them?"

"Yeah, no. I couldn't ask them," Melinda said adamantly. "Like I said, I've always felt kept in the dark on stuff. They're very secretive. I don't even feel like I know everything about Uri. I've always just figured it was a cultural thing. So, to answer you, no. I wouldn't feel comfortable asking them."

Rachel considered the situation for a second longer, and said, "We'll just have to keep our eyes on them then."

***

The rich, enticing scent of the grill filled the air signaling the undeniable arrival of summer. Rachel took a seat next to Susan Bishop at the fire pit and listened happily as fellow church members discussed the day's sermon on living a life unto God, versus a life unto man.

Susan leaned over and put her arm around Rachel with a friendly squeeze.

"These potlucks are my everything," she whispered. "I'm so grateful for you and your ability to bring people together."

Rachel smiled and watched the fire dance and crackle in the warm evening air. Just as she noted the first flicker of a fire fly, she saw Melinda, Uri, and Ivan, along with Zane and Ursula, round the back of the house. Bemused, but glad they made it, Rachel stood to go welcome them.

"Oh my," Susan gasped as if someone had surprised her.

"What is it?" Rachel asked, startled.

"Are they the Novak's?" Susan asked looking concerned.

Rachel nodded. "The whole bunch, Zane, Ursula, Uri, Melinda, and little Ivan."

Susan grabbed Rachel's hand and held it, momentarily stopping her from going to greet them.

"Oh, sweetie. We need to be careful," she said standing to go with her. "There's something dark there."

CHAPTER SIX
DARKNESS SETTLES IN

The box was heavier than it looked. The salesman who put it in the car for her must have been stronger than his thin frame suggested. Staring at it sitting precariously halfway in and out of the trunk, Rachel debated what to do. She had wanted to surprise Cody, but there was no way she was getting it in the house, let alone upstairs, without his help. Shrugging her shoulders, she decided to move on to plan B.

Loading up her arms with all of the other bags, she waddled towards the door.

"Cody?" she called, struggling to fit up the stairs.

"Yeah, babe," he responded, coming to the top landing.

With a bewildered laugh, he met her and took some of the bags. "What's all this?" he asked.

"Well," she said, pausing for effect. "I was hoping to get everything set up before I told you; but I've got news."

She pulled a stuffed animal from her bag and made it dance.

"We're going with a gray and yellow theme for the nursery," she said. "And, I'm starting on it today, *because...* we've been chosen by one of the birthmothers we selected!"

Rachel squealed with excitement as she raced to hug Cody.

"Really?" he asked, sounding unsure. "What does that

mean?"

Disappointed with his level of enthusiasm, she stepped back.

"Well, it means we have to get ready for our child who's due July 26. It also means we need to start planning our trip to Croatia."

Tucking the toy back into the bag, she added, "I thought you'd be more excited."

"Oh, Rach," he said, lovingly. "I'm just a little taken back. I'm so eager to get our family started. I'd just resigned myself to the idea it might not happen with *CTB*. It seemed like they weren't doing much. You're positive? You believe this is happening?"

"Yes!" she exclaimed. "Melinda has been so honest and straightforward with their lack of progress. I have to believe her when she says we've been selected. Of course there's still a risk that it'll fall through; but we've got to have faith. And, we've got to get ready! The crib is in my trunk. Can you help me bring it up?"

Still hesitant, Cody looked at her and nodded. "Sure, in a few minutes. I was just finishing up an invoice for a client."

"This is important," Rachel snapped. Her inflection surprised her and from the look on Cody's face, it surprised him as well.

"There's plenty of time, Rach. Plus, with *CTB*'s track record, it's probably not happening anyway. Give me 10 minutes to finish this invoice. It's due by noon."

Grabbing the bags back from him, she angrily walked towards the room that used to be hers when she lived in the house with Aunt Cali. Tossing everything in, she added, "Because, if it does go through, and we're welcoming a new baby into our home in a month…we have so much to do."

Cody looked like a deer in headlights.

"A month?" he said stunned.

"Yes," Rachel said softening. It was their first argument

and she wanted it to stop. "It's the end of June already."

"You're right. When do they recommend we go to Croatia? Prior to her due date or when she goes into labor?" he asked obviously working to get his head around everything.

"The labor's private. The hospital doesn't allow anyone in the delivery room, but we should be in town at that time. Her pregnancy is healthy, the baby's weight is good, so Melinda recommends we book our tickets for a few days prior to her scheduled due date."

"We just hangout in Croatia and wait?" he asked perplexed.

"Well, yeah. In Zagreb. It's the capitol. So, there should be plenty to do. We'll get a text when she goes into labor and then be notified once the baby's born...that's when we head to the hospital to go pick her up."

"Her?" Cody asked, his voice cracking just ever so slightly with emotion.

Rachel's eyes filled with tears. "We're having a girl."

Cody wrapped his arms around her. "I'm sorry, Rach. I love you," he said. "I just don't want to see you hurt again. I don't want to hurt again."

"Me too," she said. "We have to stay optimistic though... have faith it'll all work out."

"Okay," he agreed. "Let's go get the crib."

***

The room had become almost as inspired and sacred for Rachel as the park. Although, she feared she was giving it too much power. The way things had been going in Collinsville lately, she wondered if she shouldn't give Cody's concerns just a bit more credence. After their totally unfounded and bizarre argument, Rachel had started noticing grumpiness and irritability in almost everyone she interacted with.

At first she was concerned it was her. She thought she had done something to turn all of Collinsville against her. Racking

105

her brain while at the cafe, wondering what it could be, she saw Teresa snap at Baby Izzy. Knowing how absolutely out of character it was for not only Teresa to lose her cool; but for Baby Izzy to be challenging, Rachel suddenly recalled her conversation with Maddy.

Maddy said she felt like there was a "dark cloud hanging over the town." And, there definitely was something dark happening to Collinsville. It was impossible to put her finger on or clearly define what it was; but Rachel decided everything and everyone felt *off.*

Sitting on a cushy floor pillow in her old room turned nursery, she loved the way the morning light flooded through the windows and bounced off the fresh white walls. Buttery accents of yellow and calming gray made the space sunny and serene. It was so perfectly suited to her time of meditation, she wondered if she had designed it for herself or the baby. Gripping a soft plush bunny to her chest, she knew who she had designed it for.

A baby, she thought. A beautiful, small being; like the real life embodiment of an answered prayer. She shook her head. Until she held the little girl in her arms…no, until she was on the plane home, in the air, over the Atlantic, she couldn't allow herself to believe it was real. She needed to plot and plan to be prepared, just like taking inventory at work. But, she couldn't get into the emotional piece, not until their little girl was home.

Bowing her head and closing her eyes, she said a simple prayer of gratitude and asked for strength and peace over the next few weeks. She prayed deliberately and quickly, afraid she might fall asleep. They had booked their airline tickets for Croatia the night before, and whether it was excitement or fear, Rachel hadn't slept a wink. She was pretty sure Cody hadn't either. She felt his every toss and turn.

Forcing herself to get up from the floor cushion, Rachel prepared to head to *Cali's.* She was already nervous about taking her parental leave. After all the pressure everyone felt during her agency search, she feared things might fall apart — or explode — with an extended absence. Cody assured her that she would be spending plenty of time there. *"The baby will be constantly sleeping,"* he said. *"And, you'll be totally sleep deprived. Your only sense of normalcy will be going to* Cali's *for a cup of coffee and to check-in with everyone."*

Only sense of normalcy, she thought with a smile. *When did Cody get so tuned in to motherhood?*

She was grateful for his awareness and understanding. But, she was still concerned what would happen to *Cali's* while they were in Croatia. She would not be stopping by for coffee, or to check-in, for at least two weeks. She needed to compile a task list for people. She couldn't pile everything on Maddy. And, she figured, it would be better to have multiple people accountable for specific things. That way she would know who to check-in with about what when she did get home.

Walking to work, the birds seemed to serenade her footsteps from above. As she rounded the corner onto Main Street, she found herself just a short distance behind two boys she knew from her *Holy Rollers* skate club. Before she could say hello, their topic of conversation caught her attention and she inadvertently began to eavesdrop.

"You going to *Cx3* this year?" Nathan asked.

"Nah," Brian replied.

"Yeah, me either," Nathan agreed.

"I think my mom's gonna let me take the train to the city this summer," Brian added.

"Really? All by yourself?"

Brian nodded his head. "Yeah. My cousin lives there. So, I'll take the train to meet him."

"Lucky," Nathan said. "Is your cousin cool?"

"Yeah. He's in college. He let me have a sip of beer one time. I think if I go out to see him, he'll let me have my own."

Rachel stopped walking as her heart sank. She didn't want them to know she had heard the conversation. But, she wanted to stop it and somehow remind them how wonderful *Cx3* was. She wanted to tell them how much better it was than a can of beer, or a train ride to the city.

Hanging back she shouted giving the allusion of just spotting them. "Nathan! Brian! Hold up."

"Hi, Mrs. Brooks," they replied in unison, both looking a bit like the cat who swallowed the mouse.

"I thought that was you two," she said cheerily walking up. "How's the Collinsville summer treating you?"

"It's fine," Brian answered. "Same old, same old."

"You make it sound like you're bored already. Is there anywhere else you'd rather be?" she asked.

Nathan snickered. "Yeah, the city…or something."

"Did you know I grew up in the city?" she replied.

They both shook their heads no.

"I did. In Queens, if you want to be technical. And, do you know how I spent my summers?"

They looked at each other and then shrugged.

Rachel laughed. "I tried my best to pretend I was somewhere like Collinsville! I did everything I could to try and escape the heat, crowds, and dirt and grime of the city. But, it was nearly impossible. If you went to the community pool, it was so packed that you couldn't really swim. In the summer, the neighborhood parks got taken over by high school and college students looking for a place to drink beer and smoke cigarettes. So, it ran all of the younger kids out. I'd go to the library a lot, because it was air-conditioned. I also spent a lot of time on our fire escape daydreaming and wishing I was at my Aunt Cali's in Collinsville. I wished I was on a pedal boat in the park, eating cheesecake yogurt at *Watson's*, exploring in the woods, on an inner tube in the river, or…Oh, how could I forget? I would always think about *Cx3*. There was nothing like it in the city."

They both looked surprised. "You make Collinsville sound cool," Nathan said.

"I'm not *making* it sound cool," she said. "It *is* cool. That's why I moved here. Sheesh. *Cx3* alone draws people from all over the state. Did you know that kids bus in from Manhattan to attend? We're able to walk there. You guys'll never know how good you have it. I didn't even know what stars really looked like until I was your age."

They both laughed.

"I'm not joking. I thought Venus was a star. It's what I would use to make wishes as a kid," she said. Of course there were wonderful things about summers in New York. With the world-class concerts in the park, outdoor movies, street performers, the city seemed like one giant playground when the weather warmed up. But, there was no need to perpetuate Nathan and Brian's animosity towards Collinsville.

"Anyhow," she said with a reminiscent sigh. "I've got to get a move-on. I'm glad I ran into you guys. Meet up to go skating soon, okay?"

"Sure," Nathan said. "See you later."

"Thanks, Mrs. Brooks," Brian said.

She smiled and hurried past saying a silent prayer that their hearts would be softened and they would feel Holy Spirit's influence. She prayed they would heed His direction and know good from evil, and choose to walk in righteousness.

As she rushed to the cafe, approaching *Watson's* she slowed her pace. Something was off. The warm morning air smelled of freshly mown lawn, sugar maple trees, and the Main Street fountain; not the sweet, rich scent of handmade waffle cones. Arriving at *Watson's* front door, she was shocked to find a bright yellow piece of paper taped to the glass. "Notice: Closed by order of the Commissioner of Health and Mental Hygiene."

Rachel looked in the window to see if she could find

Watson. Not seeing anyone, she figured she would give him a call later, if he didn't contact her first. Her mind raced as to what it could be. Rats, mice, roaches? Every one of the creepy crawlies gave her the willies. She had seen *Watson's* backroom. She knew his standards were very high. Rachel could not imagine what had happened.

The door chimed as she entered *Cali's* and customers and staff began to greet her.

Rachel waved and offered smiles feeling a bit like a celebrity attempting to be incognito. She beelined for Maddy and ushered her to the backroom.

"Did the health department come yesterday?" she questioned.

"No, but did you see the notice on *Watson's*?" Maddy asked.

"Yes. Do you know what happened?"

"I heard through the grapevine it was a roach infestation. Someone also said he had containers of product that weren't properly sealed," Maddy said, wrinkling her nose with disgust.

Rachel felt her stomach turn. "I've never seen a roach back here. Have you?"

"No. You'd think if he had 'em; we'd see some too," Maddy replied, following Rachel's train of thought.

Looking around the backroom, Rachel noticed everything that could be a violation. A large coffee bag, open. A wet cloth for wiping down counters and table tops not in the proper solution. Just filled milk carafes, sitting out. Pastries for restocking the case not properly stored.

"Help me get this place in shape," Rachel said, tossing the cloth in the trash bin and getting things into acceptable storage bins.

Maddy took the carafes to the walk-in fridge and assessed what might need to be fixed there.

"What is going on?" Rachel asked, frustrated. "There's

110

got to be a mistake, right? I mean we do a good job here, but we're nowhere near as on top of things as Watson is. We miss little things occasionally, especially during the morning rush. But, I know if I go out to the condiment bar and check the milk temperature it'll be fine. I know everyone's following protocol making beverages and serving food. Whereas, Watson, he'd be able to tell you, offhand, what the exact temperature of the milk was or the mark-out date for the cookies in the pastry case, probably down to the hour. It makes no sense that he would be shut down for a health code violation. Let alone for something like roaches. I've been here for years and I've never seen a roach, a rat, or a mouse. The worst thing I've seen is a house fly."

"I told you, Rach. There's something strange going on in Collinsville. It's affecting everything."

"Well, that doesn't make me feel good," Rachel said. "I'm getting ready to leave for two weeks to go pick up my baby girl and the whole town seems to be having one of those days —perpetually. I don't like the idea of leaving for so long when things really are *off*. Who knows what sort of craziness you'll be forced to deal with."

Rachel paused. "You know what?" she added, thinking. "I think I'll ask Susan if she can help oversee things. Not like managing — that's your job — but, like HR. She can come by every day or so and see how everyone is doing, talk to people, make sure everyone feels okay."

"I like it," Maddy said. "And, I like that you've assigned everyone tasks. We're going to be fine…even if Collinsville is turning into its own version of the Twilight Zone."

"Oh, don't say that," Rachel said exasperated. "It gives me the creeps. I need to call Watson."

***

"Roaches? Really?" Cody asked, as Rachel relayed the story over dinner.

"Yes!" Rachel exclaimed. "Watson confirmed it. I called

and spoke with him. The crazy thing is, though, he's never seen a roach there in his life. It's like they just appeared at the worst time possible. He said he was very nonchalant when the health inspector arrived, because he was so confident in the condition of his shop. Some of the other minor violations that he hadn't even considered, ended up being critical violations once the inspector discovered the roaches; like improperly sealed containers. He's heartbroken and I'm panicked that the rogue roaches are going to make their way to *Cali's*."

"It's just a temporary closure, right? Can't he can take care of the roaches and reopen?" Cody asked.

"Of course. It's just that his reputation's been bruised. Plus, because his shop is such a tourist draw, he feels like he's tarnished the reputation of Collinsville. And, for those people stopping by today to find the notice on the door, it has," she said with a sigh. "But, maybe it's a good thing. Collinsville has developed a negative energy and it seems the more people from other places, like the city, discover Collinsville, the worse things are getting. So, maybe this will detour a few folks and save our sweet town."

"Ever since you mentioned praying for the kids, I've noticed a change in Collinsville," Cody agreed. "Nothing's quite as pleasant as it was just a few months ago. Everyone's grumpy and serious. It's as though everyone's having a bad day and it just keeps cycling through. Vera snapped at me the other day…for scrunching up her sleeve as I walked her to her seat at church. Vera's a bit of a curmudgeon; but she loves me. She's never snapped at me."

Rachel took a deep breath, working to calm her nerves.

"Do you think it's us? Do you think people are angry at us for some reason?" she asked. "Or, is it possible that we're being extra sensitive because we're preparing to welcome a new baby into our lives? It could be we're seeing the world through different lenses, right?"

"Sure, that's all possible," Cody agreed. "Let's just do our best to stay Christ-like. You and I should make it our priority to be as kind and compassionate as we can be, if for no other reason than to set a righteous example for our girl."

A warm breeze encircled them at their patio table, rustling the napkins and brushing at their hair. Rachel smiled knowingly.

"Holy Spirit thinks you're on to something," she said. "I do too. The plan to respond in a Christ-like, compassionate way no matter what the situation gives me peace."

"You do like structure," Cody said with a laugh. "I'd say a clear framework and justice are two of your favorite things. But seriously, I think it's the only solution. I can't imagine getting swept up in this wave of angst and animosity. It'd be such a bummer to live that way. So, while there might be a dark cloud over Collinsville, I say we make it our priority to share light."

Rachel laughed filled with gratitude for her idealistic husband. "Okay then. Project Sunshine commencing in 5-4-3-2…"

Suddenly her cell phone rang.

"It's Melinda."

"Do you think she wants to go over plans for our trip to Croatia?" Cody asked.

"I don't know," Rachel said answering her phone and putting it on speaker so Cody could hear. "Hi, Melinda. How's it going?"

"Good, good," she replied. "I think."

Rachel suddenly felt ill. She made eye contact with Cody who looked a tinge greener as well. "Why? Is it about the baby? What's going on?"

Melinda cleared her throat. "Well, yes; but more about your trip to Croatia," she replied stumbling over her words. "Oh, darn, how do I explain this? Long story short, your baby girl's on a flight coming to you now. She's with a guardian nurse and should be arriving to Collinsville around noon tomorrow."

Rachel began to laugh and cry at once. Cody just looked frozen.

"Oh my gosh. Oh my gosh," Rachel began to chant like a mantra.

"Melinda?" Cody broke-in, coming to. "Is everything okay? Why is she two weeks early?"

"Yes, everything's fine. The birthmother went into labor early. Your sweet girl was just ready to come. It was an incredibly short labor and once the birthmother spent a few minutes with the baby she was ready to let her go," she explained. "That's why you're just now being notified. We had to scramble to get ahold of one of our trusted nurses and get the travel papers in order."

Cody and Rachel were silent, stunned.

"It's not the way we prefer to do things; but it's not out of the norm," Melinda added.

"Noon tomorrow?" Rachel asked, confirming.

"Yes. Are you ready? What can I do to help?"

Rachel began to giggle, giddy with fear and excitement. "Ready?" she repeated. "We've got everything everyone says we need for a baby and then-some. But, are we ready?"

Cody laid his hands over Rachel's and leaned towards the phone.

"Yes. We're ready, Melinda," Cody stated, comforting Rachel. "Although, it looks like the little surprise event for Rachel tomorrow is toast. Do you think you could help notify people?"

"Oh, that's right!" Melinda exclaimed. "Of course. I'll get in touch with Maddy. She and I will handle it. You two...go out dancing or something...it's your last night as non-parents."

As the call closed. Rachel stared at the screen.

"The girls had a surprise baby shower luncheon planned for you tomorrow," Cody said. "They'll just have to do it once you feel up for it."

She continued to stare, pondering the situation.

"What're you thinking?" he asked.

"We're already parents," she said softly. "Do you feel it? Our girl's here, on a plane over the Atlantic Ocean. I'm not going to sleep a wink."

"Let's say a prayer, huh?" Cody suggested.

"Yes. Please."

"Lord, thank you so much for blessing us with this incredible opportunity to be parents. We are overcome with gratitude, but also responsibility, worry, and surprise. Please be with us in this time of need. Bless us with peace. Bless us with confidence so that we may welcome this little girl with unconditional love and pure joy; nothing holding us back. In your name we praise you. Amen."

The soft breeze blew in again, whipping at the tablecloth and dancing about their faces, softening the mood, and calming Rachel's nerves. Stretching, she lifted her hands to sky.

"Cody!" she exclaimed filled with excitement. "We're parents!"

CHAPTER SEVEN
SPECIAL DELIVERY

Droplets of sweat trickled down Rachel's temples tickling her face. Just fifteen minutes to noon and her breath felt sharp, hollow, as though she might hyperventilate if she didn't focus on something and just breathe deeply. It was all of 78 degrees outside, but she was burning up. She wanted everything to be perfect when she welcomed her little girl home. *She* wanted to be perfect. But, as the sweat ran down her cheeks and beaded at the top of her lip she felt anything but perfect.

"You want some water, princess?" Joe, Rachel's dad, asked laying a hand on her shoulder.

Rachel flinched at the contact. "Sure," she replied curtly, surprised and slightly defensive that he'd noticed her discomfort.

She watched apologetically as he made his way to the kitchen. He and his wife, Pam, had arrived from the city at precisely 8 a.m. with bagels and coffee from Larry's, one of Rachel's favorites. They were all welcomed reinforcements, since she had been up since 5 a.m. and had used up the last of their coffee pods. Jittery, overwhelmed, excited, nervous, and exhausted, she sifted through the bagel box for some sustenance. She hoped some carbs would help her body manage all of the caffeine and help her push through until her sweet girl was delivered.

Joe returned with a cool glass of water and Rachel accepted it gratefully, chugging it as graciously as possible.

"Thank you," she said sheepishly. "I bet you never saw mom like this."

Joe paused, bewildered by the statement. "Like how, princess? Nervous?"

"Like a sweaty, shaky, disheveled, nervous mess," Rachel corrected.

"You'd be surprised. Your mom was as graceful as they come, but she still had her moments," he said. "When she went into labor with you, for one."

"What happened?" Rachel asked. She had heard the story, but wanted her dad's take.

"She was at the market, overdue with you. We were having friends over. Do you believe it? I was such a jerk. I wanted a party, so your mom invited a few of our friends over for a special 60's themed dinner at nine months pregnant. It was over the top. She had an aspic salad in the fridge, you know, like a Jell-o thing. She was making beef bourguignon. One of the guests was bringing 'pigs in a blanket' or something, and your mom insisted that we needed Lipton Onion Soup Mix to make an authentic dip for a veggie platter," he recalled with a smile. "She was in the checkout line, soup mix in hand, when her water broke. I received a call from the corner market that I needed to come get her. When I made it down, she was a flustered ball of nerves. She couldn't stop talking about how excited she was to meet you. Even after we made it to the hospital and she started in on the most intense contractions, she would breathlessly exclaim how she was that much closer to seeing you. She was beautiful in a whole new way. Runny mascara, undone hair and all. She just exuded an entirely new energy; she was a joy-filled mother."

Rachel felt her chest tighten. She could envision how her mom felt. While she wasn't experiencing contractions, she was laboring in her own way.

"If it's any consolation," he added. "You don't look like a sweaty, shaky, disheveled, nervous mess. The only reason I asked if you wanted water, is because I wanted some."

He offered his charming smile and she laughed lightly. It felt good.

"Mom always looked so pulled together," Rachel reminisced. "I loved that about her. It was calming. No matter what we had going on, she always looked like she was ready to go out to dinner. I want to have my daughter see me like that."

"Yeah, no jeans and T-shirts for your mom. But, she would have looked like a movie star no matter what she wore. It was her poise that you were seeing, not the coiffed hair and perfect cat eye. Well, the package added a little something; but it really was her elegance that set her apart," Joe said. "And you have that."

"Really?" Rachel asked, unsure.

"Oh, princess. You've got it in spades."

Turning to look out the window again, she inhaled deeply and suddenly felt an air of calm overcome her. It was as if she'd just received a comforting hug from her mom. *Thank you*, she said in her heart. *I needed that.*

Just as she found her breath and calmed her heart rate, Melinda and Uri pulled up. They held hands as they bee-lined for the door.

Cody, who had found his own quiet, panic space in the backyard, met them at the door to let them in. Rachel was grateful to see it appeared he had received some peace as well.

"They'll be here in five minutes," Melinda announced. "How are you doing, Rach?"

"Fine, good, fine," she stammered. "Excited."

Melinda gave her a tight squeeze. "You're doing great, girl. I was basically in the bathroom at this point, splashing water on my face."

Rachel appreciated the reassurance, but felt her temperature begin to rise again as Melinda let her arm linger a little too long across her back.

"Can I get you two anything to drink?" Rachel asked making an escape to the kitchen. "We have coffee, water, juice, soda. We're basically a corner bodega."

"No thanks," Melinda replied.

"I'll take a coffee," Uri said heavily. Rachel noted that he looked exhausted and miserable.

"Uri was up all night finishing all of the legal forms for you two to sign," Melinda said, beaming with pride. "We're all so excited for you two."

From her former life as a lawyer, it surprised Rachel that there would be a need to pull a last minute all-nighter for something that she thought should be fairly routine, considering they did many adoptions from Croatia. But, not about to question it, she brushed the thought aside and looked at the clock. Three minutes.

"Thank you for working to let us receive her here, in our home," Rachel said. "I know you normally do this at the office."

She smiled and patted Rachel's shoulder. "Of course," she said. Then leaning forward with a whisper added, "There's no reason we couldn't, except for two people's fear of change."

"How're things going with the in-laws?" Rachel asked, having a terrible time focusing on the conversation. "I've been so busy getting ready for the baby, we haven't spoken about it."

Shaking her head and putting her finger to her lips, Melinda motioned for silence. "We need to talk, but not now," she said in an even softer, hushed tone.

Rachel raised an eyebrow, concerned, and nodded in agreement.

Just then a car pulled up the long driveway. "Is it them?" Rachel asked, racing to Cody's side.

Hurrying to the door to greet her new, baby girl, Rachel felt her chest vibrating with emotion. It was as though she was having an out of body experience, observing her physical and emotional reactions from afar.

"It's the Bishops, Rach," Cody said, stopping her in her tracks. Taking her hand and giving her a soft kiss on the head, he said, "I'll let them in. Did you want to go upstairs for a couple of minutes? You know, go have a prayer moment in the nursery or anything? I can take care of everyone here."

Rachel nearly burst into tears, overcome with love and gratitude for him and his idea.

"You're brilliant," she said giving him a quick peck. "Don't let me miss a thing."

"I'll come get you the instant I see them coming down the drive."

Rachel raced up the stairs and nearly dove into the nursery. The instant she was inside, serenity washed over her. Taking a seat on one of the large floor pillows she picked up a sweet little stuffed animal shaped like a bird. It had been her own as a child, a gift from her mom. She had two special dolls as a little girl, Charlie Bear and Skylark. She loved them both equally, but Charlie was the playmate, the workhorse of the pair. He would accompany her everywhere and eventually ended up quite literally disintegrating after her move to Collinsville. Skylark had always proudly perched atop Rachel's bed, keeping watch and helping to bring her good dreams.

Holding the plush toy against her chest, she closed her eyes and took in a deep, calming breath.

"Heavenly Father, You know my heart. You know my fear and excitement. Can I just be still in blessed awe of you and your goodness? Will you sit with me while we wait for my daughter to arrive?"

She felt a soft electricity run down her arms and her eyes welled with happy tears. She inhaled again deeply and listened to her heart. *Name your daughter Skylark. She will bring light and love to your family and everyone she meets.*

Rachel opened her eyes and looked back at the stuffed

animal in her lap. She smiled and wondered what Cody would think. They had planned to name her Sari, in honor of her mother Sarah.

Suddenly there was a soft tap at the door. Cody poked his head in the room. "They're coming up the drive."

Rachel pushed herself up and walked over to him. Sinking into his chest, he embraced her as they stood in silence for a moment.

"You ready?" he asked.

"So ready," she said confidently.

Taking her hand they walked down the stairs just as Melinda opened the door to let the nurse in who was carrying a large, covered baby carrier.

"Is she sleeping?" Rachel asked walking towards them.

The nurse shook her head and with a thick Croatian accent said, "No. She's wide awake and looks very eager to meet you two."

Letting go of Cody's hand, Rachel knelt down and pulled back the gauzy covering to come face to face with the most angelic face she had ever seen.

A flood of emotions overtook her as she quickly, but carefully, undid the straps to pull out the precious child. "Oh, my girl!" she exclaimed pulling the doll-sized infant into her arms and kissing her forehead. Cradling her, she stroked her small, wrinkly arm and stared into her big, doe-like eyes. The child was no more than 36 hours old, but was alert and aware, seeming to scan Rachel's face, getting to know the woman she had been waiting to meet. "Oh, Skylark, my little girl, I'm your momma. And, this is your daddy," she said turning to Cody.

"Skylark," he repeated without skipping a beat. He had tears in his eyes as he took her into his arms. "Hello, sweet girl. Welcome home."

Skylark shifted and let out a contented murmur.

"She should be hungry," the nurse said, handing Rachel a

bottle.

For a split second, Rachel panicked realizing she had never fed an infant. But, as she took a seat on the couch and Cody placed her back in her arms, Skylark seemed to lead the way, happily accepting the nipple and doing all the work. As she suckled, Rachel was able to watch in wonderment and gratitude this precious gift cradled in her arms. It was the most amazing, overwhelming, yet absolutely natural and perfect feeling she had ever witnessed. She felt completely and utterly bonded to Skylark, and she felt God's love for the both of them fill the room.

Two of His children in need of each other, bound together in love and gratitude. Little Skylark, the physical embodiment of an answered prayer. *I prayed for this child*, Rachel thought as she absorbed the moment. *Heavenly Father, you have entrusted me with a precious gift and I am eternally grateful. I am in awe. Please bless me with the ability to be the parent you want me to be.*

Waking Rachel from her trance, Cody knelt down before the both of them and kissed Skylark's tiny hand. Rachel lifted the bottle higher and he gently placed his hand under her forearm. Looking into her eyes, he whispered, "I love you. I love you both so much."

Rachel nodded, at a loss for words. Her heart felt near bursting and *love* seemed too small a word to describe the overwhelming bond she felt for the two people before her.

"Family," she said softly.

As Skylark finished the bottle, Rachel set it on the table and looked at the nurse. "Do I burp her now? Against my chest?" Rachel asked, positioning Skylark over her shoulder.

"Not like that anymore, dear. Like this," she said expertly placing Skylark in Rachel's lap and wrapping her fingers around the base of Skylark's jawline. With her hand seemingly around Skylark's neck, the nurse then showed Rachel how to properly pat her back.

"I feel like I'm strangling her!" Rachel exclaimed, concerned.

"Oh, no, dear. You are fine. This is good for the baby."

As if to confirm it, Skylark let out a soft burp followed by the most ladylike spit-up Rachel had ever seen.

"And, see," the nurse added. "If you had her over your shoulder, that would have ended up in your hair."

Watching as the nurse confidently wiped up Skylark's face and then grabbed a diaper from her bag, Rachel wished she had a little more experience for Skylark's sake.

"How long do I have you for?" she asked the nurse.

"Two hours."

"Teach me everything," Rachel asked, feeling desperate.

"Oh, Rach," Susan Bishop's voice surfaced from across the room. "I got you, girl. We're all here to help."

Suddenly Rachel realized the room was filled with friends and family. Looking around, holding Skylark on her lap, she saw nearly all of the same loving faces who had been at her and Cody's wedding at the start of this journey. People who loved her and wanted the best for her. Many of the same people who had been at her Aunt Cali's funeral and helped her cope with the loss, as well as supported her as she worked to decide whether to stay in Collinsville or return to the city.

She smiled with relief. "Okay, friend," Rachel said with a laugh. "Get over here and show me how to change this babe's diaper."

Everyone laughed and Susan excitedly joined her on the couch. Taking the diaper bag from the nurse, she walked Rachel through the process step-by-step as the nurse observed approvingly.

Pam began taking lunch orders as Joe fired up the barbecue. In addition to breakfast, they had apparently brought hamburgers and hotdogs, anticipating a crowd.

Fed and clean, Skylark yawned deeply.

"There's paperwork we need to take care of," Uri said.

"Of course," Rachel replied, looking at the baby about to fall asleep in her lap.

"Can I hold her?" Susan asked, hopeful. "Just while you get the paperwork completed, of course," she added with a wink.

Rachel handed her the tiny child and watched as she gently rocked and swayed, putting her right to sleep.

"Should we go to the kitchen?" Rachel asked. "Will the kitchen table be easier?"

Uri nodded. She and Cody led Melinda and him to the other room and took a seat. As he began to walk her through all the documents, she had memories of when her Aunt Cali died and she had an influx of things to sign, decide, and take care of. It was a lot to deal with.

Back then, all of the paperwork she had to sign and fill-out released her Aunt Cali, transferring ownership and responsibility to Rachel. Today, as she reviewed the forms and signed, listening to the soft sounds of lullabies and sweet murmuring behind her, she felt as though she was releasing ownership and responsibility. For a moment, she had a vision as if she were finally transferring ownership to God; of her life, Skylark's, and Cody's. The task before her was so important, so monumental, it would not be her, or Cody, or the community of Collinsville raising this child, but Him. And, of course, they would all be there to help.

***

"Oh no," Rachel said concerned. "What do we do?"

Cody groggy, shirtless and covered in white spit-up sat at the hallway desk, frantically surfing the internet for an answer to *newborn projectile vomit after formula,* while Rachel changed Skylark into yet another new onesie.

"It looks like I overfed her," he said, returning to the nursery. "She's okay. I think she just ate too much."

"Thank goodness," Rachel said, picking up the now perfectly happy baby and hugging her to her chest. "You can go back to bed. I'll get her down."

"You sure?"

Rachel could tell he was exhausted. She was still trying to figure out if he was attempting to win husband of the year award or was just a martyr, but he had been taking the brunt of the night feedings and little miss Skylark was turning out to be a bit of night owl.

"Really," Rachel repeated. "Please get some sleep."

She gave him a kiss and then watched as he shambled back to their bedroom, wondering if he was going to clean off his chest before getting in bed. With a shrug she turned to look at sweet Skylark who was wide awake.

Rachel giggled. "Alright, my love. What should we do?"

Taking a seat in the rocking chair, she propped her feet up on the ottoman and laid Skylark on her thighs. She loved just staring at her perfectly round face and soft, golden peach fuzz hair.

"Should we read a book?" she asked. Then glancing at the pile of books on the shelves next to her, she thought better of it. "How about a story, instead?"

Skylark held onto Rachel's index fingers as she gently began to rock.

"Once upon a time there were two sisters. Each had golden hair, the color of the sun; not unlike yours actually. Although, one had straight and the other had wild curls, and just like their hair, their personalities were similar, but different. Full of life, one chose to put it all out there. She was passionate and romantic and loved with all her heart. The other was guarded and independent and was as loyal as they come..."

Skylark had already fallen asleep. Rachel gently took her into her arms and placed her back in her bassinet and stood over her for a moment. "I'm talking about your grandma and Auntie Cali, sweet girl. I wish you got to meet them. I know they're watching over us. And, I know they're just as in love

125

with you as I am; I can feel it."

With one last look, Rachel headed back to bed.

Just as she sank into her pillow and Cody draped his arm around her waist, Skylark was awake and screaming. She felt Cody stiffen as he prepared to get up.

"No, Cody," she said. "I've got her. You sleep."

***

Rachel watched Skylark sleeping soundly through a haze of steam from the coffee cup perched at her lips. She felt blissful; blissfully dog-tired, but filled with bliss just the same. She was delirious from sleep deprivation since she didn't have the helpful kick of hormones from breastfeeding (which she learned while researching how women did this up-all-night-thing). She was running on pure joy and caffeine. But, in her delirium she was eager to get back to her prayer walk practice and share Collinsville with Skylark.

She debated pulling the sweet baby out of her crib to head off for the morning, but thought better of it. It had been a little more than two weeks, and aside from pediatrician appointments, the two of them hadn't left the house. Their doctor had strongly recommended avoiding large crowds for the first 12 weeks, so Rachel hadn't even been to church. She wondered what people did in Manhattan, where large crowds were just part of daily life, and then recalling her childhood realized people just went about their life. So, she had plans to attend this coming Sunday and cautiously keep Skylark covered in her carrier.

Cody had just started back to work, and Rachel was attempting this *mama*-thing solo for the first time. So far, so good, she thought. But looking at the clock it had only been 30 minutes since he left. Ready to feel the sun on her face and share her overwhelming gratitude with God, she looked for something to keep her occupied until little miss sleepy head woke-up. Grabbing her phone she sent a text to Maddy at work to check-in.

"How're things going at the cafe? The boutique?"

Maddy responded almost instantly, *"You get no info without pictures."*

Rachel giggled causing Skylark to shift. Quelling her laugh, she flipped through all of the pictures from the last few days and sent a small selection.

"She's beautiful. Is it weird that I think she looks like you?," Maddy replied.

Rachel responded with a smile and a question mark.

"Things are pretty much the same over here. You haven't missed a thing," Maddy texted back.

"I'm going to the park in a bit, I'll probably stop by after."

"With Skylark?"

"Yes."

Rachel's phone screen was suddenly filled with dancing, smiling, crying, heart-filled emojis, causing her to stifle another giggle outburst.

Taking another sip of coffee, she felt prompted to reach out to Melinda. They hadn't connected since a few days after Skylark's arrival; and that visit was purely professional. She had thought about her a number of times as she sat nursing the baby back to sleep, but it was always in the wee hours of the morning and felt inappropriate to shoot off a text. In the midst of welcoming Skylark, Rachel had gotten the impression there was something going on with the Novak family. And once she finally had a moment to ponder the happenings of the monumental day, she was concerned about her friend.

"Hey, friend. How are things?"

Rachel watched as the little ellipsis indicated Melinda was texting back. It took a while, starting and stopping. It seemed like she was writing and then second-guessing her response. Finally, a text came through.

"Good! How're YOU doing? Skylark?."

Relieved by her answer, Rachel wrote, *"Good. Just*

waiting for her to wake-up so we can go to the park."

"Up all night, sleep all day, right?"

"Exactly," Rachel wrote, smiling to herself. *"We should get together soon. I'm ready to rejoin society."*

"Ha ha. We're excited to have you both back."

Suddenly Skylark began to gently shift and let out a soft cry. Rachel set down her coffee and went to the crib.

"Good morning, my sweet girl," she said, picking her up. "How'd you sleep?"

She tried to intuitively guess Skylark's answer, but felt like she was still getting to know her. Taking a seat in the rocking chair, Rachel offered her a bottle and she took it happily. As they sat and rocked, Rachel gently cradled the little girl in her one arm, still amazed at how tiny a newborn actually was. Born at 6 pounds, 13 ounces, she was a perfectly average size; but the more Rachel looked at her, she was anything but average.

She had the most beautiful caramel brown hair and soft blue-gray eyes, both of which Rachel was convinced were going to stay even though it was much too early to tell. Her skin was a nearly translucent milky white, but her cheeks had the perfect blush of pink just at the apples that seemed to be getting fuller every day. She really did resemble what Rachel pictured when she envisioned an angel.

Once Skylark finished, Rachel quickly got her dressed and they headed out the door. It felt as though she had springs in her shoes. She walked to the park with such enthusiasm and excitement, it was amusing how her ponytail bobbed and whipped behind her. But as she reached Main Street the sound of loud, angry voices caused her to take pause. Just outside *Watson's* two men and their wives were bickering with one another as their young children stood looking at a quickly melting, upside down cheesecake yogurt cone on the sidewalk.

Rachel slowed and made her way to the corner to cross

the street to the park. Unsure of whether she should intervene or get Skylark out of ear shot; she was forced to stand and wait for the crosswalk, listening.

It seemed the two groups were arguing about who was responsible for the dropped cheesecake yogurt. Apparently, one child from the first family had pushed a child from the second family, causing him to drop his cone. The father of the child who lost his cone, in a misdirected attempt to defend his son, reprimanded the child from the first family, which didn't go over well with his father. So, they all stood at the front door angrily debating.

Rachel looked at Skylark in her stroller lying on her back, innocently looking to the sky.

"It's 10 a.m.," Rachel said in astonishment. "I'm sorry, sweet girl. This wasn't the side of Collinsville I was hoping to share with you. Well, it's a side that I didn't even realize existed until recently. I'm excited to show you Main Street and introduce you to Watson, among many others, but let's go to the park for now…get away from this craziness."

Finally, the light turned green and they crossed, leaving the negative tones behind.

Trying to get the disappointing incident out of her mind, Rachel began to point out all of the beautiful things she enjoyed about the walk. She showed Skylark the beautiful skyline of Eastern Cottonwood trees lining the outskirts of the park.

"No matter the season, the leaves catch the sun's rays and shimmer and shine, unlike any city skyline," Rachel said. "I always think they're the most beautiful in summer until I see them in autumn. Autumn in Collinsville trumps everything. All of the trees morph into golden, glittering versions of themselves. All of Main Street transforms with the deep hues of orange, red, and yellow. In October, the Sawyers offer hay rides on the weekends and Watson launches his special Pumpkin Cheesecake Yogurt…maybe that should be your first solid food, it would be about the right time…but it might spoil you for everything else…"

Skylark shifted and sneezed. Rachel smiled and adjusted the stroller's canopy to keep her out of the sun. As they entered the park, Rachel took in a deep breath and just enjoyed the silence for a moment. *Dear Heavenly Father,* she prayed in her heart. *Thank you so much for blessing me with the opportunity to be here this morning with Skylark. Please bless us with Holy Spirit's presence. Allow us time with Him in this sacred place. Amen.*

In a hushed tone, Rachel said, "My love, welcome to Collinsville Park. It's a very special place. This is where mommy likes to walk and spend time with Holy Spirit. I'm so grateful to be able to share it with you."

Skylark yawned, already worn out from the walk over. Rachel leaned forward and brushed a finger across her cheek. She felt the need to constantly touch her, assuring herself she was real; that she wasn't a dream. Slowing her pace she watched, filled with gratitude for such a beautiful babe, as Skylark's eyes fluttered shut and she went back to sleep. She loved this child on such a level it was nearly painful. She never imagined the bond would feel so natural or divine, so immediately. Even though she didn't give birth to her, Skylark was born to be her child. There was no doubt in Rachel's mind.

The sandy earth beneath her feet felt delightfully familiar as she meandered her favorite park pathway. Bowing her head she pondered all of the things she was grateful for, sending prayers of thanksgiving for everything that came to mind. *Skylark, the Park, Cody, Susan, Collinsville, the cafe and boutique, her life experiences, her relationship with Holy Spirit…*

Suddenly her meditation was interrupted by the sounds of a children's soccer game on one of the fields past the lake. But it wasn't the friendly sounds of good-hearted athletic banter. It was the sound of one overzealous father screaming at his child with such intensity his voice was beginning to crack.

"What is going on?" Rachel wondered aloud.

Just when it seemed he couldn't get any more fanatical, the referee blew his whistle making a call. All of the man's vitriol, and hoarse yowling, was immediately directed at the ref along with disparaging epithets having absolutely nothing to do with the game. While it wasn't completely bizarre to see such behavior at a sporting event, the man's level of intensity seemed better-suited for a professional team's playoff — not a children's summer game. But, the worst thing for Rachel was the fact that something so worldly as intense, unsportsmanlike competitiveness, especially in a children's game, had made its way to Collinsville. She had honestly thought her little town was immune to such things.

She recalled her own teenage years running track at Collinsville High. The meets, even if a title was on the line, were filled with excited cheers, positive vibes, orange slices, and icy, delicious lemonade. If the ref, or in her case a judge, made a call, it was respected and often resulted in a runner apologizing to either her team or another team. The meets always ended with one team congratulating the others with high-fives and handshakes. Rachel had attended a number of football matches in those days as well, and the good-natured sportsmanship was universal.

Disheartened and confused, Rachel took a seat on a nearby bench and gently rocked the stroller. She prayed Skylark was unable to hear the awful things as she slept.

"What's happening to Collinsville," she asked in the hope that Holy Spirit would answer. Her sacred park was feeling less than spiritual at the moment and she wanted reassurance that He was still there.

Rachel, I'm with you always, she heard her heart remind her.

Feeling a sense of calm and love wash over her, she was

relieved to know He was there, with her, even in the midst of such worldly, competitive energy. Composed, she said a prayer for the angry man, his child, and the referee. She hoped each would find the sense of peace she was experiencing and that the Lord would watch over them. Then, the need to pray for the children of Collinsville weighed on her again. She was beginning to understand the need to help them understand clearly the difference between good and evil, right and wrong. When their parents were acting as the few she had witnessed this morning, how were the children supposed to know, she wondered.

Taking a deep breath, she reverently prayed that He would be with the children and help them to see clearly and know, guided by Holy Spirit, the difference between good and evil. She realized as she prayed how easily children could misconstrue right from wrong when they were looking to flawed humans as guides. Just as she started to add her desire to be able to model herself after Him, to be a good mentor for her daughter, she heard footsteps approaching.

"Rachel?" Melinda's voice came from behind.

Straightening-up, Rachel turned to welcome her friend.

"Is Skylark sleeping? Are you busy?" she asked quietly.

"Skylark's sleeping, but we won't wake her. Come sit down," Rachel said, feeling like her friend needed her.

"I hope I'm not interrupting you. When you mentioned you were coming here in your text, I just felt like it was the perfect opportunity to talk. There's been some crazy stuff happening the past couple weeks and I'd love to get your input."

"Really?" Rachel asked surprised. "Talk to me. How can I help?"

"I feel like I should preface all of this with something; but I'm just going to dive in. Maybe put on your lawyer hat so you can listen with a real critical ear," Melinda said. "Because, there's a very good chance I've just been spending too much time with Ivan and am a little nuts from isolation."

"I can do that," Rachel said, getting worried.

"Well, as we were preparing the paperwork for Skylark, Uri was working crazy hours. He's normally very meticulous, not only with his work, but with his workspace. Everything is always pristine and obnoxiously organized. But, because things moved quicker than expected with Skylark's birth, and the adoption format changed from you two traveling internationally to personally pick her up from the mother, to her needing to be released to a nurse bringing her to you, we were rushed to figure out some additional logistics. Uri had to push through specialized travel documents for the nurse, have release documents signed by the birth mother and the hospital, et cetera," she said waiving her hand in the air. "Anyhow, I got up before him the morning after it was all completed..."

Melinda paused appearing to search for the right words.

"I started putting all the papers away and I hit the spacebar on his computer. There were two instant message boxes open. One between Uri and Zane and one between Uri and someone I didn't know. Both were in Croatian. Honestly, Rach, I've been taking that language for years and I still read like a 6-year-old, but from what I could read it sounded like there was something really questionable going on."

"What do you mean," Rachel asked, concerned. "Questionable in regard to what?"

"Ooooh," Melinda cried shaking her hands as if she was trying to rid herself of something dirty. "I think...it looked like...well, there was something about...taking babies. Like, stealing them, or buying them, or maybe both. Like, black market stuff."

Rachel felt sick. She looked at Skylark sleeping soundly, morning rays of sun shining off her white blanket, making her look particularly angelic.

"There's no way," she said adamantly. "I was a lawyer. Those forms, the process, were all very legitimate."

Touching the stroller to rock it gently, she laughed softly. "Skylark's no black market baby. I mean look at her."

Melinda folded her frantic hands together in her lap, keeping them still. "Oh good," she said softly. "See, I knew I just needed to talk to you. I really can't read Croatian for anything. I don't know what I was thinking."

"Just relax," Rachel said. "Maybe you've been watching too many mystery shows. You guys are doing good things for people. You have blessed my life so intensely, nothing I do can ever repay you. I know Ursula and Zane are tough roommates, but I do think you'd feel better about them if you stopped the witch hunt."

Melinda looked pained. "You're right, Rach, Thanks for listening. If you head over to *Cali's* you'll need to stop by the agency and say hi to everyone."

Rachel nodded and stood to give Melinda a hug. "Just relax. I would've smelled something fishy a mile away."

CHAPTER EIGHT
SPIRITUAL WARFARE

Rachel glanced at the time. Surprised by how late it was, she quickly popped a chicken tender in her mouth and grabbed a piece of cornbread to go.

"You two are so cute, I really don't want to leave," she said looking at Cody cradling Skylark in his arms.

"It's good for you to get out," he said softly. "But, you should eat a real meal. The women will understand if you're running behind. You've got a baby now; you're expected to be late."

She laughed and walked over to give them both a kiss. "I'm excited to go. I'll eat when I get home. Plus, people normally bring baked goods."

"Enjoy it. Get your spiritual, and coffee cake, grub-on," he said, laughing at his own joke.

"You're a dork. I love you. See you guys in a couple hours. Call if you need anything."

Stepping out the door into the warmth of the late summer night alone felt liberating. It had been weeks since she had been out alone. And, while she cherished every waking moment with Skylark, it was necessary for her to have personal time to revitalize in order to be the best mom she could possibly be.

The heavy humidity from the day seemed lighter as the sun descended and made her want to power walk to the church. She said a silent prayer of gratitude for Cody and his competency as a dad. She had heard people say that men were not nurturers by nature, but she begged to differ. She prayed Skylark would be blessed to find someone as great as her dad someday.

It had been nearly two months since she had been to Tuesday night bible study. She was eager to commune with the female fellowship of Collinsville Christian Church. The camaraderie and beautiful conversations always left her feeling spiritually full, which she desired now more than ever because she had really been feeling a little empty lately. She hoped spending time with solid Christian women talking about God would refuel her tank. It wasn't totally tapped out, by any means. But she was ready to feel full again.

She could see fireflies darting about a wooded area as she approached the church. Their little blinking lights were so magical. It was as if they were little guiding lights, directing her toward the filling station. *Cody's right,* she thought. *It's important for me to allow myself time to do things for myself. I have to be spiritually fed in order to provide Skylark with a righteous home.*

Skipping up the stone steps to the church's foyer, she heard loud raucous sounds coming from somewhere inside. Confused, she wondered if there was possibly a youth event scheduled at the same time. Opening the front doors, she could tell it was coming from the common area at the back of the church.

"Lila!" Rachel called out, spotting an old acquaintance. "Is Bible study tonight? What's all the noise?"

"Hi Rachel," Lila replied barely stopping. "No Bible study; bingo."

"Bingo?"

"Yep. We took a vote a couple of weeks ago. All of us had made it through the Bible. So, we figured it was time for a little break."

"Bingo?" Rachel repeated.

"Did you bring cash?" Lila asked.

"Cash?" Rachel asked feeling like she was in an episode of *Candid Camera*.

"You can't play unless you brought cash."

Rachel couldn't believe what she was hearing. Dumbstruck, she followed Lila back toward the common area to discover a large group of women sitting attentively at folding tables. In the corner Vera stood at a podium, a small metal bingo cage to her left.

"B-12, ladies," she announced. "That's B-12. Followed by...O-71. O-71."

Rachel felt a chill wash over her, completely freezing her excitement for a spirit-filled evening. She watched as Lila walked up to a desk where a sweet-looking elderly lady sat with a metal cash box. Handing her a five-dollar bill, she received a small stack of bingo cards and quickly found a free seat to get ready for the next game.

Feeling a rush of disappointment and animosity, Rachel turned on her heel and raced for the exit. As she burst through the front doors, tears began to run down her cheeks. She looked for a place to hide, somewhere to seek refuge from her overwhelming sense of darkness and despair. She wasn't ready to go home, even though it was her place of solace; she wanted answers. Looking to the woods, she saw the fireflies. Drawn to their light, feeling like all other light was dimming, she raced towards them.

As she reached the trees, she collapsed to her knees and wept. Frightened and sad, she prayed.

"God. Where are you?" she questioned, looking to the sky. "I feel so blessed, yet so far from you. You have provided me with so much. Cody is the most wonderful husband, the boutique and cafe are such a joy in my life, we've been blessed with a beautiful home, my father has returned, and now with Skylark, the immense gifts you have laid before me are truly overwhelming. But, it's almost as if they're being sent down in lieu of a deeper relationship. It feels like I'm receiving letters with money again…"

She paused, feeling like she may have gone too far and been disrespectful. How could she compare the Lord to her wayward father, she wondered. Then knowing that He knew her heart, that He understood it was just her expressing her feelings, she cleared her throat and went on.

"My Lord, I know you're there. I know Holy Spirit is with me always; but where? I feel so alone. The world feels so dark right now. I question what sort of place, what sort of town, I've decided to bring a child to….to raise our baby girl. What's happening to Collinsville? It feels like your love and light is fading here…it feels…"

She hesitated. "It feels dark here. Like evil things are moving in."

Feeling a chill wash over her again, she shivered. She looked around, suddenly frightened, and got up to head home. She walked quickly down the now darkened street, turning to look at every snapping twig and crunching leaf. Her mind raced, thinking about all of the terrible things she had seen change over the past few months in Collinsville. From her near accident with the car and angry customers at *Cali's*, to the health inspection at *Watson's* and the crazy dad in the park, she thought about how things had changed in such a short period of time. She thought about Skylark's adoption and then about her last conversation with Melinda, and she felt her stomach flip-flop.

Melinda's words suddenly rang in her ears. *Stealing babies. Buying babies. Blackmarket stuff.*

Rachel began to run towards the house.

Racing down the drive, she could see brightness shining through the windows. Sweat streamed down her temples as she ran up the steps and into the loving light of home.

"Cody?" she called softly.

She waited.

"Cody?"

Frantic, she raced through the first floor, looking everywhere in the kitchen and living room, the back patio and front office.

"Cody!" she yelled, her voice cracking with fear.

She ran up the stairs and as she reached the top, Skylark's door opened and Cody stepped into the hallway with a finger to his lips.

"I just got her down," he said softly walking over to give Rachel a hug hello.

Overcome with relief, her emotions consumed her and she dropped her head on his shoulder. Big, wet tears rolled off her cheeks onto his shirt. He held her quietly, lovingly until she calmed down.

"What is it?" he asked concerned.

Rachel wiped at her face. "Oh Cody," she said. "Tell me you thought the adoption process was totally legitimate. Tell me everything is copacetic."

He looked at her confused at first and then the color began to wash from his face.

"I feel like it was legitimate," he replied with just a beat of hesitation.

"Why'd you hesitate?" she asked.

"Well, I did feel like there were some red flags with the agency, you know? Just with how wishy-washy they were. I also questioned some of their excuses for why things were taking so long," he said. "I haven't said anything, but it also hasn't been clear to me why they all moved to Collinsville so abruptly. But, when everything was said and done, I felt like the adoption process was a success, because we got Skylark."

Rachel nodded in agreement. "But, was anything about the actual paperwork or process fishy?" she asked. "Did any of it feel fabricated?"

He seemed to review the day in his mind. "No, Rach.

Nothing about the paperwork stands out as strange or fake in my mind. But, it's not like we're experts at the process, you know?"

Her heart sank as she realized he was right. No matter how familiar she was with legal paperwork for real estate, it wasn't connected to adoption paperwork. And although she knew she was relatively acquainted with legal form protocol compared to the general public, the whole baby fever thing did not have her on her A-game, by any means.

"What's going on?" Cody asked. "What did you hear?"

She took a few steps back to take a seat at the computer desk, feeling as though her legs were getting weak.

"I've been Melinda's sounding board since we met," Rachel began. "I knew she'd been dealing with some stuff with the family. I even knew she had been suspecting Zane and Ursula of something iffy. So, when I went for my prayer walk the other day, I texted her to let her know I was heading out and would like to see her. She came straight to the park. I didn't even get 10 minutes into my walk before she arrived. Immediately, she tried to tell me about a sketchy exchange she found between Uri and Zane. It was in Croatian, so she wasn't completely confident in what it said, but she knew it wasn't good. She said there was stuff about taking babies or buying babies, maybe even stealing babies, like black market stuff. She wanted my impression. She wanted me to weigh-in. I don't think she considered my position in the whole thing. I think she was still just looking at me as a friend she could come to in a time of need. It was all too much. I blew her off. Without even thinking, I shut her down and told her there was no way. She accepted it quickly. Looking back, she accepted my denial too quickly. She realized the news was too detrimental."

Rachel wiped at a stray tear and looked at Cody.

"It's still too much. How is this even something that I'm discussing with you right now?" she asked.

Cody walked over and knelt before her.

"We'll get this figured out, Rach. Please don't fret until we have something legitimate to back this up. I mean, you said she isn't fluent in Croatian. There are a lot of things that can be misinterpreted with language, idioms, all of it. I mean, I wouldn't give the agency a great review or recommend any of our friends to them; but it's a pretty heavy charge to think that they have the ability or know-how to be smuggling babies," he said. "I just don't see Uri or Zane having the gall or intelligence. Plus, stuff like that doesn't happen in Collinsville."

Rachel sat up in her seat, attentive and angry.

"Maybe it didn't a few months ago. But things have changed," she said bitterly.

"I know we've noticed some negative influences in town coming in from the city or other tourists," he agreed.

Rachel let out a puff of air in annoyance. "Bible study is now bingo night."

"What?" Cody asked in disbelief.

"They took a vote a couple of weeks ago. There weren't even baked goods."

"Was there any sort of Biblical theme? Anything spiritual?"

Rachel laughed, trying to find a release from the absurdity of it all.

"No. Nothing Biblical, unless you consider a bunch of women sitting around praying for Vera to call B-11, spiritual," she said dryly. "Cody, there's something happening to Collinsville. And, I'm beginning to think we're caught smack-dab in the middle of it."

***

"Oh, Rachel," Susan cooed. "She's beautiful. I think Maddy's right. She looks like you. It's like it's meant to be."

Rachel shifted in her chair, uncomfortable and unsure of how she should broach her concerns with her dear friend.

"Okay, missy," Susan said taking her eyes off of Skylark and focusing them on Rachel. "What's up, something's bothering you."

Rachel let out a little laugh. "You know me too well. There's a couple of things," she replied. "First, what's going on at church? I tried to go to Bible study last night and it was…"

"Bingo. I know," Susan cut-in, sounding disgusted. "Believe me, it wasn't my idea or my choice. The ladies took a vote. If you noticed, I wasn't there. I'm a silent objector."

"But, why?" Rachel implored. "I'm sorry, but you're not silent on *anything*. Why would you object to something so obviously influenced by the adversary, silently?"

Susan looked shocked by Rachel's straightforward assertion, but then appeared to be pondering her point.

"Oh my holy night, you're right," she said after a minute. "How'd I not see it?"

"It's not just the church. It's all of Collinsville," Rachel replied. "There's something happening here."

Susan took a sip of her latte and set the cup back on the table. Looking at Rachel with a sideways glance, she began to waggle her finger and nod emphatically.

"You know what? John and I were having this exact conversation just the other night," she said excitedly. "I was saying how I felt like there was something evil moving in. It's subtle. Little negative changes here and there, but it's becoming visible. People have shorter fuses and everyone seems more interested in looking out for number one, as opposed to the community. I really noticed it at the Collinsville City Council meeting last Thursday. People were up in arms about so many things. City council meetings have always been a place of camaraderie and likeminded agendas; you know, focused on improving things for everyone. This most recent one, there was even an outright argument between Shilo, the owner of the Quik-e Mart, and Miles Goddard, the man who owns the stables just behind. They began to shove one another over whether or not a four-way stop was needed at their intersection. I'd never seen anything like it."

Susan stopped, reminiscing on the previous night's drama. Taking another sip of her latte, her face softened and she looked slightly forlorn.

"John didn't believe me," she said in a whisper. "He told me I was being paranoid and we ended up not talking for the rest of the night...he even slept on the couch."

Susan looked across the cafe wistfully and Rachel shifted in her seat, unsure of what to say. She had a tough time envisioning Susan and Pastor Bishop arguing. They always seemed so perfectly aligned. And, with their love for God, it seemed to Rachel that even if they weren't totally in agreement on something, they would be more focused on ensuring one another's happiness over their own. It didn't make sense.

"Oh my goodness!" Susan exclaimed, causing some of the other cafe customers to turn and look. "That's proof. John and I *never* argue about anything. We're so focused on each other's happiness, he puts the toilet seat down and I lift it up. We are constantly thinking about the *other*. The *only* reason we'd have an argument like we did the other night is because there's something, or *someone*, stirring the pot."

Rachel got goosebumps. She was hesitant to view them as *God bumps*, because they were testifying to the fact that there was something sinister brewing in their little town.

"What is it?" Rachel asked hesitantly.

"Gosh," Susan replied. "I think Collinsville might be under attack."

"What do you mean? Like, terrorists?" Rachel asked, confused.

"Sort of, but not terrorists of this world; terrorists on a spiritual plane," Susan said. "Satan and his dark influence could've found a spiritual opening in Collinsville...and, girl, if that's the case, we may be in the midst of spiritual warfare."

Rachel's heart sank and she looked at the table and then to Skylark.

"There's something else," she said, her voice cracking with emotion. "I have reason to believe Skylark might have been kidnapped from her birthmother."

***

"Ladies, ladies, settle down, now," Susan directed from the podium.

Observing from the back corner, Rachel silently prayed for the meeting to be productive. For the women to open their hearts and be directed through Holy Spirit in how to save their town. After their conversation, Susan launched a campaign to bring the community back together. And, with a handful of phone calls and selective home visits over just two days, she had nearly every woman in Collinsville sitting tensely in the pews talking about their experiences with the invading darkness.

Susan tapped the microphone in an attempt to get everyone's attention. The murmur of the crowd decreased until all of the women ended their conversations and turned to the stage.

Once she had everyone's attention, Susan offered her brilliant smile. It had a calming effect for Rachel and seemed to assure everyone that it was going to be okay.

"Thank you, ladies, for making the time to join us this evening," she began. "I'm not going to beat around the bush. You all know why this meeting has been called. It's time to take action to save our sweet town of Collinsville, and every single one of you is needed in the fight."

Taking the mic, she began to pace the stage.

"Every one of us has had numerous experiences over the past few months indicating a subtle change to our beloved Collinsville, but the biggest red flags are the minor changes we're experiencing in our own lives, and in ourselves. I want to ask that each of you take a moment and review your actions over the past month. Have you done something out of character? Have you picked a fight with a loved one, been impatient with a store clerk, or been overly aggressive while driving? Have you found yourself justifying negative actions to yourself or others?"

Susan paused as her voice wavered with emotion.

"I know I have. It's not like me at all to get annoyed with anyone, but I know just the other week I was snippy with a hotel clerk while I was traveling. I left having gotten what I wanted, but embarrassed by how I achieved those results. But, I found myself justifying my actions. Telling myself it was necessary for me to stand up for myself. *I was paying good money to stay at the hotel and deserved to be taken care of.* Another instance was just the other night Pastor Bishop and I had an argument over nothing. We never bicker and this silly disagreement resulted in him on the couch and me crying myself to sleep. I tell you these personal things, ladies, because I believe that each and every one of you has had a similar experience lately. It is the influence of Satan. He has found an opening in our sweet, little town and is working to turn our safe haven into a place of anger and sadness, aggression and self-importance, contention and depression, and, it isn't us. It is not excusable. We are all better than this. Collinsville is known for three things: our beautiful park, cheesecake yogurt, and Collinsville Community Church. We are a Christ-centered community and we are all women of God. The world has plenty of ladies who are embittered, coarse, rude, and vain. We are special because we're filled with compassion for our families, friends, and community. We need to remember we are not women of the world, we need to fight Satan's influence and be loving, faithful, tender, virtuous, and good. We need to be women of God. A wise man once said, 'With self-justification of petty sins, Satan triumphs.'"

Rachel felt her chest heave as she felt a wave of emotion hit her. She, herself, had been so caught up in her own needs over the past few months she had absolutely been impatient and dismissive with others. She hadn't been herself. And, in the midst of that discontent, she had lost a sense of joy and forgotten to come before God with everything.

Susan continued, "My dear ladies of Collinsville. As women of God, we need to fight Satan's influence over our community and protect our town. We need to pray! We need to pray as if our lives depend on it."

A roar of applause came from the audience as a warmth and light filled the room. Holy Spirit was in their midst and everyone felt His presence.

Tears flowed as the women turned to their neighbors offering apologies and hugs. Rachel raced forward. Noticing her, Susan stepped down from the stage and took Rachel into her arms.

"Thank you, girl," she said giving Rachel a strong squeeze. "You opened my eyes. We're going to save this town."

"He's here," Rachel said, through tears.

"Yes, He is. And He loves you, Rachel. You're one of His chosen daughters. There's some crazy stuff going on in town. And, I know you feel caught in the thick of it with your concerns about Skylark, but He's with you always. Through Him we'll get through this."

"Thank you," Rachel said. "I needed that."

Susan gave her another tight squeeze and then got back on stage.

"Ladies, you are all a blessing! Truly amazing sisters in Christ. I knew you'd receive this inspired message. Now, let's do this! Matthew 18:20 says, *'For where two or three gather in my name, there am I with them.'* We are more than 100 strong! He's here with us. Let's bow our heads and fight this darkness!"

Women stood, holding hands, heads bowed. Rachel found a place in a row next to Vera and took her hand in hers. She felt a current of electricity run through her body from where their palms met to her heart, and in that power there was a strength she had never felt before.

"Our Lord, our dear, gracious Heavenly Father," Susan prayed. "We come before you, united as women in Christ. We know you are with us. We can feel your presence, Lord. Please hear our plea to defend Collinsville from the evil powers that be. Strengthen our community members, safeguard our public spaces, and secure our borders from the enemy's influence. Please empower us and provide us with immunity from his temptations. Give us the strength to withstand his pressure and the ability to stay vigilant. Lord, work through us to save Collinsville. Allow us to be your righteous army and defend this special place from the enemy. Please keep Collinsville filled with your goodness and light. We love you, our Lord and King, in your name we praise you. Amen."

The group sighed a collective, *Amen*. As women around them began to gather their things and talk to their neighbors, Tamara, a young single mother who Rachel recognized from church, but found to be extremely shy, began to hum softly next to her. Picking up on the tune, Ida, a talented singer, started in with the lyrics, "Day by day, and with each passing moment, strength I find, to meet my trials here. Trusting in my Father's wise bestowment, I've no cause for worry or for fear."

Other women joined in, repeating the first verse. By the time they reached the second verse, a full choir of voices filled the chapel, singing praise with such ardor, it could have been mistaken for a battle cry. "He whose heart is kind beyond all measure, gives unto each day what He deems best. Lovingly, it's part of pain and pleasure, mingling toil with peace and rest. Help me then in every tribulation, so to trust

Your promises, O Lord."

As the singing came to a close, Susan walked through the crowd offering hugs and imploring the women to go home and pray with their families, and to get everyone to church on Sunday when Pastor Bishop would bring a very important message.

After the meeting, Rachel stayed to help Susan put the chapel back in order. As they checked the pews and stacked the additional folding chairs, she felt her burden and concern for Collinsville had been relieved. With most of the community on her side, her worry for the town was shared and the weight dispersed. But, with the release came a more focused fear of losing Skylark. Suddenly consumed with dread, Rachel worked silently until she couldn't stand it.

"What if I do discover that Skylark isn't legally mine, what do I do?" Rachel asked, almost thinking out loud. "Or, what if I don't discover it, and someone else does, and the authorities come and take her away?"

Susan hoisted a chair up to the top of the stack as anxiety and questions flooded Rachel's mind.

"What if I discover that she was literally kidnapped and her birthmother is looking for her? How do I willingly give back my daughter?"

Susan took Rachel's hands and led her to a nearby pew. Taking a seat, she looked her deep in the eyes.

"Rachel, sweetie, you can't do this to yourself," Susan said.

Rachel could detect the sincerity in her voice.

"It isn't going to help you, or Skylark, if you're filled with fear and what-if's. Second Corinthians 12:9 and 10 say, 'But He said to me, "My grace is sufficient for you, for my power is made perfect in weakness." Therefore I will boast all the more gladly about my weaknesses, so that Christ's power may rest on me. That is why, for Christ's sake, I delight in weaknesses, in insults, hardships, in persecutions, in difficulties. For when I am weak, then I am strong,'" Susan quoted. She paused and patted Rachel's hand. "Yes, the prospect of losing Skylark is frightening, but you're not there yet. You need a lot more information before you can decide whether or not to be in fix-it mode. All things are possible in Him. Please, go home and pray, hold your girl tight, and pray some more. Now is not the time to let your mind run free. You must give your fear and worries up to Him and have faith that He knows how best to handle it. You must silence the what-if's, and doubt your doubts; don't doubt your faith."

Rachel nodded weakly. "You're right," she agreed, feeling encouraged after a moment. "I need to get my imagination in check. I'll go home and pray. I also need to talk to Melinda. And, maybe, I'll give an old lawyer friend in the city a call...I know someone who might be able to help."

"There you go, girl!" Susan said jumping to her feet. "It's time to call in the big guns. And, even through we've got God on our side, help from a big time New York City lawyer never hurt anyone."

CHAPTER NINE
BUYING BABIES

"Oh, Rachel. I'm so sorry I've got you tied up in this mess," Melinda cried. "I don't understand how this is my life!"

Rachel sat silent on the park bench, unsure of how to answer. If she was being honest with herself, she was too angry to respond. Her fear and sadness had quickly been overtaken by mama-bear protective-mode, and Rachel was ready to fight-off anything or anyone threatening her sweet Skylark. And, while she tried hard to not outright blame her friend, it was a challenge for her to understand how Melinda hadn't noticed anything questionable sooner.

Taking a deep breath, Rachel said a silent prayer for compassion and felt a wave of calm come over her. She touched Melinda's arm.

"It's okay. I know you didn't know. Now, tell me what you've figured out. What's got you so upset?"

"Rachel, you can't tell *anyone*," Melinda said.

Rachel debated how to respond to the request for secrecy. She didn't want to make any promises she couldn't keep. If Melinda's appearance was any indication of how bad the news she was about to relay was, Rachel felt unprepared. Her skin was sallow and her typically bright eyes were dark and sunken. She looked sick. Following up her silent prayer, she asked for strength and guidance in managing whatever news came her way.

"Talk to me," she coaxed.

Melinda shook her head. "I mean it. You can't tell anyone. We're in this together. If anyone finds out, you'll lose Skylark, and I'll lose everyone."

The news struck Rachel's heart like a poison arrow. It burned and the pain seemed to radiate throughout her chest, spanning down her arms. Biting her tongue to keep from crying, she nodded.

"I understand," she replied.

"I did some digging and found out more," Melinda began. "From what I gathered, no one at the agency is outright *stealing babies*. They aren't in the business of kidnapping; but they aren't opposed to purchasing babies with muddy backstories or without legal paperwork. I was able to figure out enough, that I finally had to approach Uri."

"You spoke to him?" Rachel asked, surprised.

Melinda nodded aggressively, holding back tears.

"Yes," she said. "The other night, after I put Ivan to bed, and Ursula and Zane were at the other end of the house. I sat with him and...just asked."

She took a breath and continued, "He was mad at first, angry that I'd gone through his personal correspondence and business papers. He started to yell at me and tell me I was crazy. It was so out of character. But, I didn't get upset, because something inside made me think he was really scared. He continued to yell for a minute and then he just stopped and apologized. He gave me a hug and said he should've come clean a long time ago."

Rachel was on the edge of her seat. Melinda paused to blow her nose and organize her thoughts.

"He said he had found out in a similar way two years ago," Melinda continued. "He'd been helping his dad on a case and needed some information late at night, so he went into Zane's computer to grab it. He came across an exchange between his dad and a man he'd met in Croatia. When he asked his dad about it the next day, Zane lost it."

Melinda took a breath and wiped at a stray tear. "That's why he stopped yelling at me. He realized he was reacting the same way his father had. Anyhow, Zane made him feel terrible for questioning him and Uri ended up just dropping it; feeling as though he had misjudged the situation. But, over time, his dad started to feed him information and before he knew it, he was in over his head. I mean, he's in over his head…we're all in over our heads."

Rachel bristled at the assertion. Always a champion for justice, a lover of honesty, she despised even being included in the conversation as a potential participant. Looking around, she tried to escape into the beauty of the park she loved so much. It bothered her that they'd selected this sacred place to discuss such a dismal matter. She could feel the anxiety building as she waited for Melinda to continue, and a little voice in her head asked her if she wanted to hear more. *You're going to keep Skylark no matter what; why do you want to hear any of this and potentially incriminate yourself.*

For just a moment, the lawyer in her entertained the thoughtful legal advice, then recognizing the voice of the adversary, she shoved it down.

"Please, Dear Heavenly Father, help me," she petitioned silently. *"Help me to deal with this in a manner that pleases you. I know you'll help me through."*

She turned to Skylark, who had been peacefully napping in her stroller throughout the conversation. The sweet girl suddenly shifted and raised an arm. Outstretched, with a tight little fist resting above her head, it looked as if she was claiming victory. Rachel smiled, and decided to take it as a sign that it would all work out. A soft breeze blew past, again calming her nerves and enabling her to sit still, be patient, and listen.

"Fill me in. I still don't know what anyone's done wrong. You've got me on pins and needles," Rachel encouraged.

"It's just so heinous. They're buying babies. They're buying babies from moms who need drug money. They're buying babies from women giving up their babies willingly. They're buying babies from anyone who offers them a baby... regardless of whether or not they're the child's guardian. Zane, and now Uri, create false documentation and get the babies out of Croatia as quickly as possible, so no one can change their minds. Your situation was not unique. They always do it that way...make you think you're going to Croatia for a legal adoption, and then last minute smuggle in the newborn with a *'nurse'*," she said using air-quotes. "It didn't start this way, though."

Rachel's ears were ringing. She felt as if she'd been hit over the head with a mallet. *What was Skylark's story?* she wondered. *What had her poor, sweet girl been through in her first days here on earth?*

"What do you mean?" Rachel asked dryly. "How'd it start?"

"It started in the 90's during the Croatian War of Independence as a legit operation. Over the duration of the war, there were so many people displaced, hundreds of thousands, and nearly 10,000 children lost parents. Ursula and Zane were feeling completely trapped by the war. Zane had lost his job as a photographer. He used to do family portraits, weddings, big corporate events, but once the war started no one was looking for a photographer for that sort of thing. Uri was just a toddler and they were desperate to bring in money; but also wanted to make a difference. They wanted to help their countrymen and save themselves. Ursula had gotten a part-time janitorial job at the hospital in Zagreb. She noticed all of the child welfare workers coming in to collect children, presumably to take them to institutional-type orphanages. She talked to Zane. They both spoke English and had contacts in the United States from studying abroad in their earlier years... one of whom just happened to be the marketing director for a big, international adoption agency in New York," Melinda explained. She shrugged and put her hands up. "I'd heard the story many times before. It's one of the things I admired about Zane and Ursula; turning a dark time into something positive and up-lifting. Even through my issues with them and work frustrations over how seemingly disorganized everything was, I would always refer to their story and believe I was doing something good. I believed the agency was founded on goodhearted principles and, even though we were looking to run a profitable business, that we were giving back to humanity in some weird way."

"What happened?" Rachel asked. "Was it all a lie?"

Melinda shook her head.

"No. The agency really did start with good intentions. And, for a long time, at least all of the 1990s, they were running a legitimately well-intentioned business. They set up an agency in Zagreb and partnered with a number of their friends to get it off the ground. They had a good thing going. They were finding orphans loving homes, providing well for their family, and giving their friends' families a leg-up as well. In 2003, they moved to New York to better handle the U.S. side of the operation; at least that's what they say," she said, burying her face in her hands. Lifting her head slightly, she continued, her voice muffled with the side of her palm against her lips. "But, this is what I found out from Uri. The reality was, after September 11, there were much stricter guidelines in place, even for infant immigrants. Plus, at that point, their business practices had already started to get a little shady. There was a big U.S. demand for Caucasian babies, and with the war long-over, the pool of needy Croatian orphans was dwindling. They were desperate to keep the business running, so they developed a plan with their business partners to find children and infants wherever they could. They'd move to the U.S. to oversee that all of the necessary paperwork and documentation was taken care of, while their friends back in

Zagreb kept a constant stream of babies in the pipeline."

Rachel took a deep breath. Her bones seemed to be rattling, as if they were set to vibrate. "Did he say anything about Ivan?" Rachel asked. "Or Skylark? How'd we get our children? Are all of the adoptions frauds? Or are some of them legitimate?"

"Some have to be legitimate, I believe," Melinda said hesitantly. "Oh, I don't know. I didn't ask. I didn't even think to ask. I was so overwhelmed by all of the new information. See, though? We can't tell anyone. There's a very real chance our children will be taken away."

"Do you know anything else?" Rachel asked, feeling her inner-lawyer emerge. "Did he give you any other information? What about the move to Collinsville? What was the catalyst? Remember, you overheard Zane and Ursula talking about it being a good place to hide out. What are they hiding from? It seems like there may already be someone on to them, in which case it might behoove us to talk to the authorities."

Melinda shook her head adamantly.

"No, Rachel. Absolutely not," she said gripping her hand with enough force she was tempted to pry it away. "I'm not sure why they moved the agency to Collinsville. I assume it was just precautionary. People out here are…trusting, and a little naive."

Rachel took her hand back and straightened her posture.

"The people of Collinsville are open and kind; but this isn't some podunk town filled with gullible, simpleminded country folk," Rachel asserted. "Definitely not so much so that I'd bet my family on it. My advice to you, Uri, Zane, and Ursula, would be to not abuse Collinsville's openness or underestimate its friendliness for being unaware or ignorant."

Melinda nodded. "I didn't mean anything negative. People here, they're just different from people in the city. They lack the cynicism. They're not as quick to look for or find fault."

"That's only because people here assume other people

want to be good, and do good things. If someone, or a group of *someones*, chooses to not be good, they'll be seen for who they are. It's only a matter of time."

Melinda sheepishly nodded, catching Rachel's insinuation. For a fleeting moment, Rachel felt bad, but then Skylark woke and began to cry with hunger pains taking her attention. Rachel reached in the diaper bag and pulled out a bottle. Taking her daughter in her arms, she placed the bottle in her mouth and gently stroked her cheek.

"You need to find out more information," Rachel added. "I need to understand what we're working with."

"You won't say anything?" Melinda asked again.

"No, I won't say anything," she said with surety. "But, I need more information."

As if they'd just shook hands, Melinda patted Rachel's thigh. "Okay. I'll talk to Uri tonight. I'll let you know what I find out."

"Okay," Rachel said not turning from Skylark.

"Well," Melinda replied, awkwardly looking for something else to say.

Rachel didn't see a need to drag out the conversation. For now, they really didn't have anything else to talk about. It wasn't like they could simply discuss the weather when both of their families were on the line. Plus, Rachel was already busy thinking about who she could contact for help and how to manage the ridiculous situation with integrity.

"I'm going to make some calls," Rachel said honestly. "I won't say anything incriminating, but I need to contact some people who might be able to help, should we need them."

Melinda shot her a look.

"Believe me. I know how to get information without giving it."

Melinda put her hands to her knees and pushed herself up to leave.

"Please don't make me regret saying anything," she said

in a tone that Rachel found ever so slightly threatening.

Choosing not to acknowledge it, Rachel continued to look at Skylark willing herself to fix this situation.

"Just let me know when you have more info," she said softly.

Melinda turned to leave and Rachel watched her walk away. As she turned the corner, heading toward the park's exit and out of view, a soft breeze blew in again tossing the corners of Skylark's muslin blanket and flipping Rachel's hair about her shoulders. There seemed to be a peacefulness that entered as she left. It was almost as if she not only carried with her bad news, but an intangible darkness. Rachel felt a shiver run up her spine and she gripped Skylark just a little tighter.

***

Rachel stared at Cody from across the patio table. She desperately wanted him to make eye contact, but he was consumed with Skylark.

"Cody?" Rachel insisted. "Nothing? No reaction to the conversation I had with Melinda?"

He looked at her and then back at Skylark.

"I never thought I could love this girl as much as I do, especially so quickly," he said softly. "The moment I took her into my arms, she was our daughter, my little girl; a living, breathing answer to a prayer. It wasn't just emotional; it was chemical. It was as if we were her birthparents."

Rachel waited quietly as he shifted Skylark to his other arm to reach across the table and hold her hand.

"I hear you, Rach. I believe *CTB* could potentially be working in some really deplorable stuff. However, there are a few things we have to remember. One, regardless of anything, Skylark's our responsibility; for whatever duration of time, we've been entrusted with this beautiful daughter of God. It's our duty to fight for her and protect her, and to act in her best interest, even if her best interest is not *our* best interest. Two, we have resources. We have time, money, friends — you in particular have friends in high places — and, we have our Heavenly Father. We've got what we need to do whatever we have to in order to make this right. Lastly, everything Melinda's told you is hearsay. She's been on a witch-hunt since you met her. Plus, the fact that she's even talking to you about this really incriminating information makes me feel like she's a gossipmonger and has a slight penchant for drama. I've got to assume it's not as bad as she says it is."

"I think I'm going to call Tom, if that's okay with you," she blurted out. She had only talked about her ex a handful of times with Cody. It wasn't that Cody had any sort of issues with her past, it was just once Rachel left Tom, quit being a lawyer, and moved to Collinsville, she finally felt as though she'd found her place in the world. Tom quickly became a fuzzy, distant memory. And, once she and Cody were an item, she never looked back.

"His uncle is District Attorney Pierson. I feel like they might be able to help us," she said.

"*The* District Attorney Pierson?" Cody asked, impressed. "Like, of the state of New York?"

"Yes, that one," Rachel replied. "He and I always had a good relationship. I just don't know what the Pierson's think of me since I left Tom...with a phone call. It was terribly uncivilized and they're all about civility, and manners, and etiquette; among other things."

Rachel threw her hands in the air.

"They always say it's a bad idea to burn bridges," she added. "The only reason I'm even considering it, is because when we broke-up he sent flowers and a nice note; nothing mushy or desperate. Just a simple card that read, 'You will be missed.' And, we were together for a long time. I think if he needed something, I would help him...I think."

"Of course you would," Cody said. "Because you're the type of person who wants to help people. Let's look at this from his perspective. You and your husband — who isn't him — need help keeping their adopted daughter, who they've potentially adopted on the black market and may still belong to someone else in Croatia."

Rachel paused. The words rattled in her ears and she felt a gush of wind whip by. It wasn't the calming, peaceful presence she had come to recognize as Holy Spirit. It was filled with fervent emotion and was meant to get Rachel's attention. Replaying Cody's words in her mind, she accepted this was more than just finding a way to keep Skylark and make sure everything was status quo. They needed to find Skylark's birthmother and make sure she had actually, legally put Skylark up for adoption.

Looking at the precious little girl in Cody's arms, Rachel was suddenly filled with compassion thinking there could be a mother out there who had lost the child she had spent nine months carrying, loving, eagerly anticipating, and giving birth to.

"There's maybe someone out there, maybe a young couple like us, wondering what happened to their little girl," Rachel said, her voice wavering. "I have to try reaching out to Tom. I don't know how else we'll have the ability to truly investigate this and make it right."

Cody looked down at Skylark and stroked her head.

"Are we really capable of making this right? Someone, potentially us, is going to end up heartbroken," he said.

"We have to try," Rachel said, her stomach turning as her heart felt stronger than it had in a while. "Like you said, we have to act in Skylark's best interest, and we have God on our side."

Cody nodded and scratched at his scruffy jaw with his free hand.

"For lack of a better term," he started. "Let me play devil's advocate here. There's a good chance Skylark was obtained legitimately. Possibly sold by her birthmother for money. Or, maybe given up for adoption for good reasons. There's also a chance she wasn't. Maybe Skylark was acquired illegally; maybe sold by the hospital where she was born, the nurse telling the mother she died due to complications, or maybe she was outright taken. Regardless of the circumstances of how *CTB* came to have her, do you believe with all your heart, she would be better off back in Croatia, than here with us?"

Rachel was shocked by Cody's response.

"Rach," he said kindly. "I'm with you on this. It's imperative that we choose to do what's right. But, I'm just realizing we're going to be up against a lot. It's not only going to be us hurting people who we know by working with authorities to bust their illegal crime ring, but it's also going to be us battling ourselves, our hearts, and the little voices that crop up saying we are doing the *wrong thing*."

Rachel draped her arms across the table and reached out to him and Skylark in frustrated exasperation. Cody reassuringly stroked her forearms.

"We can make it through together as long as we stay focused on Him," he added. "Through the guidance of Holy Spirit, He can help us to see clearly our own weaknesses and quiet those unreliable inner voices."

Rachel felt *God bumps* break out up and down her arms. Nodding, knowingly, she said, "I know those confusing, conflicting voices all too well. They're the adversary breaking in where he sees an opportunity and he does everything he can to capitalize on times like these to make it hard to hear Holy Spirit...or to know with a surety. We have to stay united in this. It's going to be hard."

***

Rachel held her breath as the phone began to ring. By the time it reached the fourth ring, she exhaled relieved, and prepared to leave a voicemail.

"Tom Pierson," a familiar voice unexpectedly came across

the connection.

"Tom!" Rachel responded with an awkward amount of enthusiasm. Working to tone it down, she added, "It's Rachel...D'Angelo."

"Rachel," he repeated, suddenly sounding just as thrown-off. "This is a surprise."

"I'm sure," she said, wondering if she should give her married name. "I apologize for the unexpected call."

"No need to be sorry there," he tossed in, regaining his wit.

She flinched knowing there were plenty of other things she could probably be apologizing for.

"Well, I'm actually calling because I was hoping to schedule a meeting. I was just going to call the office and schedule with the secretary, but I thought I should connect with you first. Make sure you would be willing to meet with me."

"After more than two years, I'm getting a business call, huh?" he said, sounding perplexed.

"Yes. I completely understand if you don't want to. But, I've found myself in the middle of a pretty big situation that I believe you might be interested in...as well as be able to help me with," she said trying to pique his interest. "But, I'd like to discuss it in person."

"Tuesday, 9 a.m at Starbucks," he said. "I can give you 30 minutes, max."

"Thanks...," she began, but stopped realizing he had already hung-up.

Even with the abrupt good-bye, Rachel smiled gratefully knowing he was on board. She felt a small pang of guilt wondering if she was misleading him in any way. She should have given him her married name, she thought. Shaking her head, understanding his help was a necessary part of the plan, she got over it.

As she placed her phone back in her pocket, it rang.

Frightened it was Tom second-guessing their meeting, she was relieved to see it was Susan.

"Hey there," Rachel answered.

"Hey, girl! We're planning a prayer circle for this afternoon in the park. Would love to see you there."

"I'll be there," she said happy to hear the church community was continuing to mobilize. "What time?"

"Great, 3:30 p.m. at the pedal boat dock. Excited to have you, and Skylark, I hope?" Susan replied.

"Absolutely," Rachel confirmed. Her meeting with Tom still fresh on her mind, a thought popped into her head. "Hey, what're you doing Tuesday?"

"Sounds like something with you, girlfriend," Susan replied cheerfully. "What's up?"

***

"Coffee, check. Music, check. Legal documents, check. I think we're ready to roll!" Susan exclaimed with an unnatural amount of energy for their 5:30 a.m. call time.

"Thank you for joining me, Susan. I haven't seen Tom since the night I received the call from the hospital that my Aunt Cali had a stroke. His reaction was the catalyst for our breakup and I followed suit by ending it over the phone. While I don't have any bad blood, I'm not totally sure how he feels. And, more importantly, I want to be respectful of Cody," Rachel explained as she started the car. "He completely trusts me and is happy that Tom's willing to meet, but having you there with me will be great support on so many levels. This could be an interesting meeting."

"Sweetie, let's say a prayer first?" Susan requested. "Before we head anywhere."

"Of course," Rachel replied, grateful for Susan's early morning clarity.

Susan took Rachel's hands in hers.

"Dear Lord, as Rachel and I prepare to head to the city and meet with Tom, please open his heart. Should he have hard feelings, soften his sentiments toward Rachel. Allow him to be accepting of her newly married life and let him have compassion for her and Skylark. Fill him with the desire to help us and enable him to do so. Help us to be discerning and in tune with Holy Spirit so that we may make the best decisions on Skylark's behalf. We're so grateful to have gotten this far. Help us on this journey to find the information and tools we need to continue forward. Please watch over Rachel and me on our trip. Keep us safe and mindful of you in all that we do. We love you and praise you. Amen."

"Amen," Rachel echoed.

"All right. Let's jet," Susan said.

***

Time passed quicker than Rachel expected on the drive. Susan was filled with interesting stories from her many mission trips abroad, working to build churches in India, and schools in Africa. They talked about different ways to continue the momentum in the movement to save Collinsville, discussing different events and ways to get even the secular community members on board.

"Do you think this…what we're doing…could affect our progress?" Rachel asked.

"What do you mean, sweetie?" Susan replied.

"Well, let's say Tom does decide to help me. And, let's say the Novak's are running an illegal adoption agency trafficking in stolen babies. I've got to imagine there will need to be some sort of *stake out* and then a big bust leading to arrests. I just wonder if that'll be completely discouraging to everyone. Especially since everyone's fighting so diligently to rid the darkness and bring light back into town."

"I see what you're saying," Susan said. "But, if it plays out the way you've proposed, I think everyone will see it as a win. Think about it. Maybe the Novak's coming to town was part of the influx of darkness? Maybe the fact that Collinsville was vulnerable and had small cracks being filled by the

163

adversary paved the way for the Novak's to find a place in town? There's spiritual warfare all around us, Rach. Good battling evil. There are places filled with light and love, that are safe havens...like Collinsville has been, and *will be* again...and, there are places where the adversary has found a stronghold. You can tell. The instant you walk past, or enter, your skin crawls and your senses are on red alert. Those of us filled with God's light are particularly sensitive and it makes it easy to feel it isn't a place you want to be. Then there are places, like the city, that are most likely being bombarded by both sides in a quite literal, constant battle. Where good and evil are just vying for opportunities to save and destroy, respectively. So, with that in mind, if the Novak's are found to truly be doing bad things, and are rounded up and carted off, it will feel like Collinsville has had a victory in our war against evil."

Rachel had *God bumps*.

"I don't know that I'd ever heard it explained that way," she said. "It's terrifying."

Consumed with the magnitude of the concept, she took a second to digest it. The idea made her emotional.

"In regard to the Novak's," Rachel continued. "It makes sense. If they're working in such dark things and justifying so many lies, there needed to be not only an opening for them to be able to come to Collinsville, but also they would've needed to connect with something in Collinsville for them to feel like it was the right place for them to be. It wasn't like they were looking for love and light, a feeling of community, or fellowship; they wanted a place to hide out where they could keep going about their despicable business."

The whole idea, no matter how otherworldly it might sound to some, seemed to sum up the craziness in her life and Collinsville over the past six months so succinctly, she had to let it sink in a bit. Pulling up to an all-too-familiar corner, she was grateful to spot a parking space along the curb just a few feet away.

"Is this the one? *The* Starbucks?" Susan asked.

"Yep," Rachel said with a sigh. "This is it. We're early."

"Only by 30 minutes. Should we head in and grab some food, and more caffeine?" Susan suggested.

"Sounds good to me," Rachel said, her stomach starting to go sour with nerves. "I'd love to find a good table to get situated at before he arrives."

At 8:55 a.m. Rachel found herself fidgeting and watching the door. She hadn't prepared herself for how strange it would feel to reconnect with Tom and that time in her life.

"Rach?" Susan said. "It's going to be fine, sweetie. Remember why we're here. It's got nothing to do with your former life and everything to do with your current one. Holy Spirit's with us, girl. It'll all work out, just wait."

Rachel felt a warmth surround her as though someone had just come up behind and given her a hug. Knowing it was Holy Spirit, she said a silent prayer of thanks and felt her nerves relax just as she saw Tom walk through the door.

Dressed to the nines, he looked even more *Pierson* than he had when she was with him. Rachel stood and waved. Giving her an acknowledging nod, he got in line to get a coffee before coming over to greet her. She gave Susan a sideways glance and she smiled seeming to understand that this was typical behavior when he wasn't needing to impress anyone.

Eventually he sashayed over and offered an obligatory smile. "Hi, Rachel Brooks," he said extending a hand.

He had done his homework she thought as she met his hand with hers. "Hi, Tom. Thanks for the time. This is my dear friend, Susan Bishop."

Susan stood and shook Tom's hand and then they all took a seat around the small cafe table.

"You've got me, I'm interested," he said directly. "If it's brought you from the country on an errand to see me on business; it's got my attention for...20 minutes."

Rachel smiled gratefully. "We won't need that long."

"All right, then. Let's hear it," he prompted.

Rachel cleared her throat and let it spill.

"I got married a little more than a year ago. And, quickly discovered I can't get pregnant, at least without a lot of intervention. Decided to adopt. Vetted a number of agencies here in the city. Decided to go with *CTB International*. They work to place Croatian newborns with U.S. families. All seemed well and good. Started looking at profiles and every birthmother profile of interest had some story as to why we couldn't work with her or why she pulled out of the program, et cetera, etc. Finally, we were connected with a birthmother. Never actually spoke with her, but she 'agreed,'" Rachel said using air quotes. "...to having us as her baby's adoptive family. We booked our trip to Croatia to head out for the birth of our future child, only to find out that the birthmother had gone into labor early and a nurse was bringing our baby straight to us. Within 32 hours we were parents to a baby girl. Just for context, I'll say the child is perfect in every way and we are very much in love. Fast-forward a month. One of the women from the agency, whom I've befriended, has started to confide in me about how she's discovered the agency — which consists of her husband, father-in-law, mother-in-law, and a few people in Croatia — are acquiring babies illegally. While the agency started off as a legit business in the 90's during the Croatian War of Independence, they have resorted to buying babies from people and bringing them without any sort of paperwork. According to my friend from the agency, they're knowingly selling stolen babies. This agency had been located in the city until about two months ago when they relocated to Collinsville, where I live in Upstate."

"I know where Collinsville is," Tom interjected. "Go on."

"It appears they made the move to either shake someone who was on to them, or proactively ensure no one would catch on to them. From what I've heard, my experience was not unique. It's the agency's MO to be evasive and come through at the last minute so families don't have time to ask too many questions or look into things too much. Additionally, they've got a professional acting as a nurse smuggling the newborns in from Croatia. I'm hoping you and Matt will be willing to help me investigate this agency and ensure this doesn't happen to any other family. My personal interest is in finding my daughter's birthmother. I need to know if she knowingly and willingly put her up for adoption."

Tom took a sip of his coffee.

Rachel sat back in her chair and shot a relieved smile at Susan who winked back. She was grateful she'd been able to succinctly lay out the facts without getting emotional or rambling about unnecessary emotional stuff. It would have only annoyed Tom and diminished his interest.

Looking around the room, Tom's rigid shoulders seemed to dip ever so slightly.

"My mom was really angry with me when you left," he started.

Taken aback, Rachel froze for a moment. The only person in the world Tom loved more than himself was his mother. He adored her. If he was able to do something to make her proud or happy, he was like a 6-year-old showing off a gold star report card. Her acceptance meant more than anything. Rachel grabbed Susan's hand under the table for support.

"You mean she was angry with me?" she corrected.

"Nope. She was angry with me. She knew it was my fault," he admitted. "When I asked her why she was so mad, she said, 'Rachel would've been the best mother to my grand babies.'"

Rachel felt her eyes widen. Susan squeezed her hand.

"Anyhow, sorry to hear you can't have kids of your own," he said, then immediately switching gears, added, "I think I might be too engrained in real estate law now to even remember what I studied in school, so I don't know how much help I'd be. But, I see Matt tonight. I'll see what he says. We're done?"

"Yes," Rachel said.

Tom stood and shook both of their hands. Rachel had to refrain from gushing with gratitude. She knew it wouldn't help her case. Tom was much more willing to help her as a counterpart as opposed to a sniveling, scared mom, even though that's how she felt.

"I'll be in touch," he said, buttoned his suit jacket and walked out the door.

CHAPTER TEN
FRIENDS IN HIGH PLACES

Rachel sat back and rubbed her eyes. She hadn't spent this much time pouring over legal text or reviewing white papers since she was in school. Even when she was at the firm they had legal assistants to help with the most tedious research. Stretching, her chair squeaked and she froze, worrying it might wake Skylark or Cody. She waited for a minute. Not hearing a sound aside from crickets and cicadas, she returned to the dense documents, searching for the proof she needed that her adoption papers were fraudulent.

District Attorney Pierson had agreed to help, if — and only if — Rachel could supply him with the proof he needed to get a search warrant. She had to admit *CTB International* was good at falsifying documentation. It made her sad they would spend so much time perfecting their art of deception as opposed to finding children who really did need adoptive families.

Reviewing everything in front of her, she let out a soft, yet frustrated, slow breath.

"It's not here," she whispered.

Then she saw it — an overview of the Hague Adoption Convention and a clear outline of how child laundering worked. There is no paper trail she realized. The children are kidnapped or purchased or sold to an orphanage acting as a front. The orphanage pays a fee for the child and then turns around and sells the child for a profit. This meant that she and

Cody were most likely safe. But, what did that mean, she wondered. The adoption in the eyes of the US was legal, but what was it in the eyes of God? If she worked to prove Skylark was obtained illegally, did she risk losing her? Again, a voice in her heart said she had to do what was right.

Reviewing what she learned, she knew the proof wasn't in the legal documents. They were all legitimate. The proof she was looking for had to stem from the Novaks themselves. It hadn't escaped her that the quickest and easiest way to a search warrant would be to record Melinda the next time they spoke, but she couldn't bring herself to do that to her friend. It was one thing to find a mistake in the paperwork, something that anyone, if they looked hard enough could discover. It was another thing to record her friend incriminating herself and her entire family.

Rachel looked at the clock, it was 2 a.m. She had to go to bed. Even though Skylark had been starting to sleep for longer stretches, Rachel needed a decent night's sleep to be a mom, a wife, a storeowner…and a human.

She scooted out of her chair and got on her knees.

"Father, please help me to figure this out. Help me to find the proof I need to provide Matt with the impetus to investigate *CTB*. And, please help me to find something without having to outright betray Melinda's trust. Thank you, Lord. I'm eternally grateful to have you to turn to in times like these. Amen."

As she crawled into bed, she could tell autumn was coming. There was a chill in the air. Cuddling close to Cody, he woke slightly.

"You're staying up too late," he said.

"I know. I'm sorry to wake you."

He rolled over and embraced her. She loved the way he smelled like sawdust and soap. It was a unique mix of musky freshness that was very manly and very Cody. Drifting off to sleep, Rachel ran through all of the possible places she might find the bit of evidence she needed.

***

"Good morning, night owl," Cody said, handing her a cup of coffee.

Rachel yawned and gave him a kiss. "Thank you, I need this more than you know."

Realizing he had Skylark in a wrap on his chest, she began to giggle.

"You're making coffee and wearing Skylark?" she asked with a laugh taking a seat at the island. "You're like super mom! Well, putting me to shame at least."

He walked over and gave her a shoulder massage.

"Let's go for a walk, huh?" he asked. "The weather's turning and it's really crisp and beautiful outside. I think it could do us all some good."

"That sounds perfect, as long as I can get my coffee to go."

As they stepped outside, Rachel was struck by the brisk autumn morning.

"No Indian summer for us, huh?" she remarked.

"It might warm up again, but I love it. I'm ready for fall," Cody said.

Rachel snuggled in close to him as they walked.

"Me too, I think. But, this year's just flying by. I hate that I've been preoccupied with all of this…*stuff* since the moment we welcomed Skylark into our lives. I feel like I haven't been able to give her my full attention."

"You're doing really well," Cody replied. "This situation is like nothing most people have to deal with and you're holding it together and getting it figured out. You're amazing, Rach. Really. I'm so proud to call you my wife and I know Skylark is proud to have you as her mom. We both feel good knowing that you're the one going to bat for our family. Speaking of which, did you find anything last night?"

"Not much. It's crazy to think they've spent so many

171

years perfecting their fraud, when they could've been putting those efforts toward building a legitimate business," she said. "I wish I would've been more aware of the issues of child laundering before deciding to adopt abroad. Ultimately, what *CTB* is doing isn't totally unheard of. The fact that people like us are willing to pay so much for a baby makes a really lucrative motivator for people in poverty-stricken countries. And, the US has no real stance on it. Well, they don't consider it human trafficking because it isn't exploitative. The babies have no recollection of their birth family and there's no paper trail, so as long as the US-based adoption agency is operating *legitimately* and *isn't aware* of any human rights violations, they are working in a legal sphere," she said, adding emphasis to *CTB*'s most errant offenses. "That's the thing though. *CTB* knows what they're doing. Our adoption's 'legal' as long as no one knows *they* know what they're doing. Me blowing it out of the water, could cost us our baby girl."

Cody gave her a reassuring squeeze.

"I'm not dwelling on that though," Rachel added. "I actually just needed to say it out loud, but I'm not even thinking about it or worried about it anymore. The Lord has directed me to do what's right and I believe that to mean, we need to bring *CTB* to light. I have faith He will watch over us and Skylark."

"I've had the same confirmation as I've prayed," Cody replied. "I believe it'll all work out."

Rachel looked up. She had been so focused on their conversation and huddling close to Cody and Skylark, she hadn't given much consideration to where they were walking.

Just above their heads was the Collinsville Community Park sign. Her heart leapt. Cody smiled at her knowingly.

"We could both use a little meditation here," he said. "I thought it would be good to do it together."

She gave him a kiss and then nuzzled her nose against Skylark's barely visible forehead tucked inside the wrap.

Cody took her hands in his and bowed his head. Rachel followed, closing her eyes.

"Father, we come before you this morning as a family. We are bound together in love for each other and for you, and we need your guidance. Fill us with Holy Spirit's presence this morning. As we spend time reflecting on all you have done for us, show us how to ask the right questions and please reveal the truth to us. Bless us with the knowledge and courage to do what's right. Show us how to bring Your light back to Collinsville. Empower us to have the willingness and ability to do what you would ask of us. We're so grateful for all you provide. We love this little girl. We love Collinsville. We love You with all our hearts and want to do the right thing. We want to make you proud, Lord; even if it means going against what appears to be the easier choice or what our hearts want. We ask this in Your name, Amen."

Rachel opened her eyes to morning rays shining through the tall poplar trees. The light bouncing against the tiny green leaves highlighted the first hint of autumn gold that sparkled in the soft breeze. Following the sunbeams to the lake she could see someone out for an early morning ride in a pedal boat. She couldn't help but smile thinking back to her miraculous experience the year before in the park with Holy Spirit.

"Shall we walk?" Cody asked.

Rachel nodded and took his hand.

"Just so you don't think I'm weird, when I prayer walk I just meander through the park and talk with Him; silently," she said. "I tell Him all the things I'm grateful for and then I offer up the things concerning me, that I need guidance on. Once I've poured out my heart to Him, and feel I'm in a proper place — you know, hungry for His direction, open to actually *listening* — I try to quiet my thoughts and open my heart to His response. I don't always get a response, but often I do...as long as I'm truly listening. That's why prayer walks were such a challenge when I was baby crazy. I couldn't quiet my thoughts. I was too wrapped up in what I thought I needed."

Cody stopped and looked at her.

"I'm excited to prayer walk together, but I don't want to cramp your style," he said with a sweet smile. "If you'd rather be alone, we can meet up in a bit?"

"No," Rachel said adamantly. "I'm so happy to be here together, as a family, in prayer."

"Okay," he replied letting her lead.

She held Cody's hand loosely as she guided him and Skylark down her favorite path. Focusing on the warmth of his palm, the sound of gravel crunching beneath her shoes, and the laughter of children in the distance, she was able to calm her mind and block out the many mental distractions vying for her attention. As she began meditating on the things she was grateful for, a flood of positive things filled her mind. So caught up in her battle against the dark forces invading Collinsville and her personal life, she hadn't allowed herself time to pause and recognize the wonderfully positive things happening at the same time.

Her heart filled with warmth and love as she considered Cody's companionship, Susan's friendship, Skylark's existence, Tom and Matt Pierson's support, Collinsville's united front, her team at *Cali's*, and the beautiful moment that was happening right now with her husband and daughter. She felt awash in the golden morning light, as though she could see the divine love of Heavenly Father shining down on her, and through her, from her head to her feet. She felt grounded, strong, and ready to face the challenges before her.

As they rounded a corner, Rachel could see the lake again. From where they were walking, the man in the pedal boat appeared to be smiling from ear to ear as he glided leisurely across the glassy water. Rachel smiled to herself as she prepared to transition her prayer. Turning her thoughts to her many concerns, she silently placed them before God.

As each question arose in her heart she envisioned lifting it up and placing it before Him. *Dear Lord, I'm terrified of losing Skylark, but I want to do right by you. I feel filled with faith even though I am frightened by what the future may hold. Enable me to move forward confidently. Allow me to find a way to provide District Attorney Pierson with the information he needs to investigate* CTB.

I feel lost and sneaky, and concerned that I may be causing more harm than good. I want to protect other families from dealing with what Cody and I are dealing with. I want to protect other children from being treated like objects to be bought and sold. And, I want to protect Collinsville from CTB's *dark business practices. Please help me to see this situation through your eyes, allow me to be altruistic in my decisions, and help me to stay strong in my faith.*

Rachel took a deep breath and exhaled slowly. *Dear Heavenly Father, please be with us. Guide us. Protect us from harm. Shelter us from the darkness. Help us to stay positive and focused on your will.*

Strolling by her favorite tree in the park, where she dedicated her life to God seemingly forever ago, Rachel set her questions before the Lord. Quieting her heart and mind, she let go of the concerns, knowing they were in His hands, and waited. Continuing to focus on Cody's warmth, his and Skylark's presence beside her, the ambient sounds of the park, and the soft crisp morning breeze, she emptied her mind of all other distractions.

Watching the man on the lake, her mind drifted to her time with Holy Spirit just the year prior. He had comforted her, enabling her to find peace as she struggled to come to grips with Aunt Cali's death. Offering gratitude for the experience, Rachel continued to wait as best she could, redirecting her mind as it tried to wander.

Enjoy the morning with your family, my girl. It will all

work out.

Stunned by the response, Rachel snapped out of her meditation and looked at Cody. *It will all work out* was one of his lines.

"Did you say something?" she asked.

"No," he replied with a smile. "Did you hear something?"

"Enjoy the morning with your family," Rachel repeated. "It will all work out."

Cody's smile went crooked, momentarily perplexed. He then began to laugh causing Skylark to stir in the wrap. Rachel smiled and put a finger to her mouth, motioning for Cody to keep it quiet as she caressed Skylark's cheek.

"He called me 'my girl,'" Rachel said. "I love that. We truly are His children. He wants to help us, take care of us, just like we want to take care of Skylark."

Rachel paused for a moment contemplating.

"Oh, no," she suddenly gasped. "Did I interrupt your prayer? I didn't even think that you might be deep in conversation with Him. I'm sorry, Cody."

"Rach, this is a group effort. I'm glad you shared immediately. I had a subtle impression a little bit ago, but I questioned whether it was Him or just me talking to myself," he said with a chuckle. "Now I know with confidence that it was Him."

Rachel was instantly giddy with excitement.

"What was your impression?"

"'Keep it up. It will all work out,' He said. But, He didn't call me, *my girl*," he said giving Rachel a squeeze.

"What a blessing," she whispered. Taking in a deep breath, she let it out slowly, calming her nerves. "How awesome to know we're on the right track and to have even greater conviction because we both received an answer. I'm so relieved."

"Well, let's do as we're told," Cody said. "Enjoy the morning together, right?"

***

Rachel sat in the living room anxiously awaiting Melinda's arrival. She had invited her over after the morning in the park in the hopes of creating an opportunity for helpful information.

With Skylark napping upstairs and Cody in his workshop, she tried to use the momentary time to herself to check numbers at work. Maddy was doing a wonderful job holding down the fort while Rachel tried to take her maternity leave. Better communication, as well as scheduling, seemed to help the *Cali's* team members not feel overwhelmed or overworked. But, unlike when she was traveling to the city a lot looking into adopting, Rachel checked in on her employees often.

She glanced around the room. She recalled when she came home from high school to discover her Aunt Cali had filled the room with purple and white balloons in celebration of her acceptance to NYU. The memory made her smile. When she heard a knock at the door, her smile faded slightly and she prepared to try and talk things out with Melinda.

"Hi," she said greeting her at the door, and welcoming her with a hug. "Come in. How're things going?"

Melinda looked disheartened, but offered a weak smile. Rachel felt as though she could see the weight of her guilty conscience hanging on her shoulders. There was a darkness surrounding her. Rachel flipped on a few more lights as she ushered her to the living room.

"Good...I'm good," Melinda replied. "Better, I guess."

"Well, that's great," Rachel said. "What's changed?"

Melinda looked annoyed.

"Nothing, that I know of," she said with a sigh. "Uri and I haven't really talked much lately, which is why things feel fine and normal, I guess."

"So, you haven't found out anything more?" Rachel asked.

Melinda shrugged.

"Well, I've been doing some research," Rachel said. "From what I've figured out, it seems that it's a practice in some countries, like Croatia, to launder babies. Basically, babies are sold to orphanages for a sum of money. The orphanages create a new paper trail for the children and then sell them to agencies like *CTB* for a much larger fee. There have been international safeguards put in place that are supposed to protect families, children, and well-meaning agencies against this, but it's hard to control...especially when U.S. agencies are looking to negate the safeguards put in place. From what I understand the U.S. policy is to look the other way, as long as the agency is acting in good faith, and unaware of the baby's origins."

Melinda perked up. "Rachel! That's amazing news," she exclaimed. "We're off the hook. Right? We just need to make it clear we had no idea of the babies' histories."

Rachel was surprised by her response. The Novaks' dishonesty had gotten her into her current predicament. Rachel couldn't believe she would want to continue on with another lie to protect them.

"But, you *do* know. And, it sounds like Uri and Zane and Ursula are helping to orchestrate the laundering," Rachel said. "Wouldn't it be better...feel better...to stop lying?"

"Are you kidding?" Melinda asked without skipping a beat. "I have to lie to save my family. And, you do too."

Rachel bit her tongue to avoid saying anything else incendiary. She said a silent prayer for patience and the ability to communicate in a way that would put Melinda at ease, not on the defense. Not only did she sincerely want to help guide her friend down a path that would eventually bring her peace; Rachel wanted the information she needed to get Matt and Tom involved.

"I'm sorry," Rachel said. "I didn't mean to be self-righteous or dismissive of your position, I just know that throughout my life, no matter what the consequence, it's always felt better to tell the truth. I can see this is hurting you and I'm trying to pull from past experience to offer advice. But, honestly, this is unlike any situation I've ever been a part of. I don't know what the right answers are."

Melinda nodded and Rachel could see tears welling in her eyes.

"I don't know if I believe that," Melinda said. "I don't know if I believe telling the truth, or *coming clean*, feels better. I thought because I was now looped into what was happening, that Uri would be more open with me. I thought he might talk to me more, maybe even confide in me...I mean, I'd like to have the opportunity to try and persuade him to *not* be involved in this anymore. We're not thieves and we're definitely not kidnappers, but ever since I found out and he was upfront about what was going on, he's been completely shut off. He won't even make eye contact, let alone talk to me."

Rachel paused for a moment, trying to be considerate with her response.

"Do you think it's because he's ashamed?" she asked softly. "Do you think he's ashamed because he knows you think highly of him? Maybe he feels as though he's stooped below your high regard for him? The fact that he's avoiding eye contact makes me think he's embarrassed in some way."

"I don't know," Melinda said. "It doesn't make sense. We've always been such a team. From the moment we met at work all those years ago, he's had my back and I've had his. We work well together. It makes sense to me why there was a distance between us while he was dealing with this on his own, getting caught up in his dad's business. Obviously he was trying to protect me from getting involved. Now that I'm involved, it doesn't make sense to me why he would be so closed-off. I mean, he told me everything. He was so open. I thought we were in this together now."

"It's like you just said, though. You guys aren't thieves. You're not kidnappers. That's how you view yourself and that's how you view Uri. I have to imagine that's how he views himself, too. However, when it comes down to it, he's been caught up into a business that's making him justify questionable actions to himself. He may not be an actual thief or kidnapper, but he's definitely helping to facilitate; even if it's just by supporting his dad. He might've been able to find a way to convince himself that he was just following orders, or keeping his family's business afloat before, when it was just him and his dad, you know? Especially because his dad was condoning it. But, now that you know and are concerned about how the business can affect your family, with the risk of losing Ivan and everything, Uri has to be having a more difficult time justifying his involvement and everything in question. He has to be having a hard time defending his role in clearing papers for potentially kidnapped babies, when he doesn't want to believe in himself as a kidnapper."

Melinda looked stunned. Rachel retreated back into the couch fearing she'd said too much. She so badly wanted to be honest with her friend, try to get her on board with coming clean; but she didn't want to push her away or sound sanctimonious.

Rachel leaned forward and looked Melinda in the eyes.

"Look, I'm not trying to be preachy. It's important that we look at the big picture. This is not the time to be defensive or reactive. We're clued in, but on the periphery. Together we can see the situation clearly and we need to do what's right, not just for our families, but for all the other families working with *CTB* willingly or not. We've got to think long-term sustainability, not immediate, short-term protection, you know? By staying silent, you might be protecting Uri from getting in trouble with the law at this moment, but what about the stress on his conscience? What about the near future when someone eventually finds out and he's so deep in the business there's no way he'd be acquitted of wrongdoing?"

Melinda turned and looked out the front window thoughtfully. After a minute she turned back to Rachel and offered a slight head tilt that Rachel couldn't quite read.

"The last time Uri and I spoke, when he told me everything, he gave me this," Melinda said holding out a sheet of paper. "It's a print-out of the latest conversation between Zane and his business partner in Croatia. The man runs an orphanage in Zagreb. It's exactly like you were saying, they've been using it as a front. And, apparently he's in the position to acquire another orphanage in Dubrovnik. This exchange talks about 'eliminating the issues with supply.'"

Rachel took the paper and started to review the email chain.

"It's in Croatian."

"I know. Uri read it to me. I've been re-reading it and realizing that my Croatian isn't nearly as bad as I thought. I guess the news I've been reading has just been worse than I wanted to believe," Melinda said pulling the paper back. "I don't know why I showed you. It's just so awful, and I feel so alone in it all. I wanted to share with someone."

She looked back out the window.

"You're right," she added. "It's like he already feels too deep to get out. Or maybe he feels obligated to his father. I'm not sure. But, he's definitely finding a way to justify this to himself...because it's not in his nature to be deceptive or corrupt. When I met him at work, he wouldn't even take home office pens or stationery. Anyhow, I see your point, but we need to find a way to protect our families now, as well as in the future."

Rachel was disheartened by her response, even though she was relieved Melinda was listening.

"I'm not sure how to do both," Rachel replied. "I'm going to have to think. In the meantime, is there a way you can start talking to Uri? You have to put subtle pressure on him to stop.

If nothing else, you need to express your disapproval. Just so it's clear to him that you aren't on board. It will make it more difficult for him to justify it. I feel like this is an important step for the long-term protection of your family. Who knows? Maybe if you persuade Uri to stop, Zane and Ursula will see the error of their ways, too?"

Melinda squinted at Rachel critically.

"It's harder than you'd think," she said. "To talk to Uri when he isn't talking is like talking to a wall."

"I believe it. But, he's got ears. Even if you only get a sentence or two in before he walks out of the room or asks you to stop, he's going to hear your disapproval. And, I believe that's enough. You don't need to push or pick a fight; just gently let him know you don't approve and that you know he's better than this."

"You're such a lawyer," Melinda said with a smile. It was the first sincere smile Rachel had seen on her face in months. "But, it's good advice. As long as I'm not forceful or moralizing about it. If it's coming from a place of concern for him and our family, which it is, I think he'll listen. I hope he'll listen."

Suddenly Skylark's gentle cries came over the monitor.

"It's time for her afternoon snack," Rachel said standing. "You're welcome to stay. I just need to get her bottle and feed her."

"No, I'm going to head out. Thank you, Rachel. I appreciate the advice," Melinda said gathering her things and heading toward the door. "Oh, just to be clear, we're still not telling anyone about this. You can't tell anyone."

Rachel's heart sank as she started for the kitchen, hearing Skylark's cries gain in intensity.

"I understand," Rachel replied, unsure of anything else to say.

"I'll let you know how it goes talking with Uri," Melinda said. "See you soon."

Rachel waved as Melinda shut the door behind her and left.

***

"Hey, Rach?" Cody called from the living room.

"Yes, my love," she replied coming down the hallway from the kitchen. "What's up?"

He was sitting on the floor against the couch giving Skylark time on her tummy and cheering her on as she worked to lift her head.

"What is this?" he asked holding up a sheet of paper.

"I'm not sure. Where'd you find it?" she asked as she approached.

Taking a seat on the floor with them, Rachel took the paper from him. As she reviewed the sheet, she felt a warmth wash over her and her ears began to ring, at a loss for words.

"Where was this?" she asked again.

"In between the cushions on the couch, it was sticking half way out. What is it?"

She looked at him with wide-eyes and grabbed his hand with excitement. "It's the evidence we need for Matt and Tom."

CHAPTER ELEVEN
CONSEQUENCES

As the train raced along the tracks, Rachel gripped Cody's hand tightly. She felt nauseous. For the past few mornings, she had woken up needing to race to the toilet. In her heart, she debated whether they were doing the right thing. It felt sneaky. Not only did it feel like she was betraying a friend, it felt like she was embarrassingly good at it.

The instant Cody discovered the printout from Melinda, Rachel had raced upstairs to make a photocopy, in addition to taking upwards of nine photos with her cell phone. It was as though she knew Melinda was on her way to retrieve the evidence. Just mere seconds before they heard a knock at the door, Rachel had tucked the paper back in the cushions where Cody had found it. While Rachel ran around doing her undercover work, Cody supportively cheered on Skylark's tummy time achievements and her efforts, whenever appropriate.

She and Cody had both played dumb when Melinda arrived at their doorstep. In hopes she would not suspect their disloyalty, Rachel had kindly led her into the living room and allowed her to find the paper herself; acting surprised when she found it sticking out of the cushions.

"Sorry to disturb you guys," Melinda had said looking at them both as though she had swallowed something distasteful. "I really needed this paper. I can't believe I left it."

"I'm glad it was here, and not somewhere else," Rachel replied unsure of what else to say.

Now, as Cody, Rachel, and Skylark made their way to the city to meet with Matt and Tom at Matt's stately New York City office space, she felt a little uneasy, and queasy. Neither she nor Cody had slept very well. A night of tossing and turning, filled with concern and anxiety (and a handful of prayers), had made them decide to take the train to the city for fear of falling asleep at the wheel. She didn't feel prepared or mentally strong enough to be presenting information that not only was going to drastically affect Melinda's family, but could impact her own as well.

"Are we doing the right thing?" she asked, turning to Cody.

Stifling a yawn, he patted her leg. "I think so. It sure seems like it," he said. "There's no way Melinda would have left that paper without divine help."

"It just feels like we're doing something terrible," she replied.

"By telling the truth?" Cody asked.

"It feels like there's a bit of tattling involved," she said. "Yes, I want to tell our truth. I want to be honest and open with *our truth*, but Melinda is obviously not ready to be honest and open with her truth. But, by default, we're telling her truth, too. I just feel like a rat is all."

"I understand what you're saying," Cody said reassuringly. "It'd be one thing if what they were doing didn't directly impact others. If it was a victimless crime and only involved them, we wouldn't be in the position we're in, you know? But, in order for us to protect our family and legalize Skylark's adoption, as well as try to protect Croatian babies and other American families from *CTB*, we have to tell. To use your term, we have to rat them out. We don't have time to wait and see if Melinda will come around. The longer we wait the more people who get hurt, including the Novaks —

because there may be a point they see clearly the harm they've caused. In the end, if they have remorse, then the less damage they've done, the better off they'll be."

Rachel nodded in agreement, knowing he was right. She was still uncomfortable though. She kept checking her phone, thinking by some miraculous twist of events Melinda might call or text having *seen the light*.

Then, to top off her apprehension about turning over the evidence to Matt and Tom, there was the whole meeting with Matt and Tom…and Cody and Skylark. Her first meeting with Tom had been challenging and bittersweet. She was unsure of how to feel about introducing him and his uncle to her new husband and daughter. If it had been solely up to her, she would have chosen to do the meeting on her own, but once Melinda left the house Cody instantly started talking about how they would handle the trip to the city together. Rachel was grateful to have his support, even if it might make things slightly more awkward.

Looking out the window as they zipped through Upstate New York's countryside, Skylark asleep on her chest, Rachel said a silent prayer for strength and peace. She knew in her heart they were doing the right thing. She knew all the uncertainty and fear cropping up was the adversary trying to make her question herself. She didn't want to give him an inch more. As she prayed to God with her whole soul, she almost instantly felt serenity wash over her and was suddenly completely steadfast in their mission.

Overall, her emotions felt markedly different today than they had over the past few months. It was as if they were the result of some external force as opposed to her own internal conflict. Both the anxiety and calm within her were seemingly directed by unseen things in her immediate environment. As she prepared to close her prayer, she felt prompted to ask for divine protection from the adversary and his attempts to make her doubt herself. She requested protection for Cody and

Skylark, and Collinsville, as they all worked to return God's light to their home and their lives.

Cody put his arm around her shoulders. "I love you. We've got this."

It was exactly what she needed. Rachel snuggled into his hold, let her head sink into his arm, and closed her eyes.

***

"I can't believe I fell asleep," Rachel exclaimed as they made their way from the train to the Subway.

"Hey, why don't we just take a cab?" Cody asked, looking skeptical at the morning crowds racing past.

Rachel caressed the precious bundle wrapped against her chest. "It's likely to take too long, and there's a risk of getting stuck. The 4 express will get us downtown quicker," she prodded. "It seems crazier than it really is. It's safe."

Cody cautiously followed as Rachel led the way through Grand Central Station. The wait on the platform was short and they soon were sitting in a quiet subway car racing towards their destination. The scent of wet earth, electrical fumes, and city grime brought back so many memories, Rachel had to stretch to try and lighten the weight of it all.

"Do you want to grab a coffee or anything before we head in to meet them?" she asked as they approached their stop. "We'll come out of the station just across the street from the D.A.'s office. There are two Starbucks, a tiny park, a couple of other places to grab a snack, if you want. We'll have 10 minutes or so to spare."

"A coffee'd be great," Cody agreed. "I'm hurting. Glad we took the train in. I'm going to need to nap on the way back."

Stepping into the bright morning light after being underground for 20 minutes and on the train for the past few hours was inspiring. It was a beautiful fall New York morning. The skies were a pristine azure blue and large, friendly white clouds floated above seeming to skim along the many downtown skyscrapers. Rachel knew this part of town well. Just a bit south of where her and Tom's place had been, they frequented the neighborhood often to meet up with friends after work and on weekends.

She knew they were just up the street from Freedom Towers. When she and Tom started dating, the first few times they came to visit his uncle, it had been Ground Zero. City Hall was just up the street and they were within walking distance to Wall Street and Battery Park where they could catch a great view of the Statue of Liberty...if they weren't both so tired.

They ducked into the first coffee spot they saw and Rachel bounced with Skylark while Cody grabbed a cup. Her nerves and nausea just couldn't take the jolt no matter how tired she was. Taking a quick seat in City Hall Park, Rachel pulled Skylark out of the wrap and fed her a bottle. The sun felt good and having gotten a little nap on the train, Rachel was coming around, feeling better. She double-checked the diaper bag to ensure she still had the copy of the exchange between Zane and his business partner in Croatia.

Tucking Skylark back into the wrap, she turned to Cody. "Ready?"

"Let's do it," he said.

***

District Attorney Pierson and Tom entered the meeting room with an entourage of people.

A few different scenarios had run through Rachel's mind as they waited at the large, heavy wooden table, but a small conference room suddenly filled with eight to 10 city officials, herself, Cody, and Skylark, hadn't been one of them.

"Good morning, Mrs. Brooks," Matt said, shaking her hand. "It's been too long."

"Thank you for your time," Rachel replied emulating Matt's official demeanor. "I believe I have the evidence needed to look into *CTB International Adoption Agency*."

She passed the copied printout to him and explained what it was.

"If this says what you've said it does, then this will work," Matt said.

Rachel glanced over at Tom who sat quietly next to his uncle. She offered a quick, friendly smile. The only reason he was in the room was to oversee the meeting. To ensure she received the time and attention the case needed. He gave her an acknowledging nod.

Reviewing the document as though he could read Croatian, Matt picked up the paper, shoved it in his leather-bound planner and extended his hand again. "Thank you for bringing this to the attention of the state of New York, Mrs. Brooks. Hope you and your family get a chance to enjoy the city. It's a beautiful day."

With that the large group emptied the room and Cody and Rachel stood to leave. As they stepped out the door and headed toward the lobby, Tom stood just across the hall waiting.

"I'm Tom Pierson," he said extending a hand to Cody.

"Nice to meet you," Cody replied, gripping Tom's hand strongly. "Thank you for helping us. I know we wouldn't have received the same time and attention without your support."

"Is this Skylark?" Tom asked, turning to Rachel.

"Do you want to see her?" Rachel asked, a little surprised by his interest.

He gave an almost unintelligible head dip of affirmation. Rachel reached inside the wrap and pulled the wide-eyed little girl out, cradling her in her arms.

"She's so tiny," Tom replied, looking. "I don't think I realized babies were so small."

"Well, she's only a month old," Rachel replied.

"Huh," he said, seeming to consider what that meant.

"So, what now?" Rachel asked in regard to the case. "Do we just wait?"

"No. Don't even think about it," Tom said. "It's with Matt and his team now. He's up for re-election soon. If your printout says what you've said it does, Matt'll be right on it. For him to break-up a New York-based child laundering ring will bode very well for him in the polls."

"That's it? He doesn't need anything else from us?" Rachel asked surprised.

"That's it."

"But, what if Skylark's part of the child laundering? How do we deal with that?"

"Unless a birth mother comes forward with proof, there isn't need to worry. Matt will only be focused on shutting down the agency and the criminal orphanages."

Rachel felt a simultaneous wave of consolation and concern wash over her.

"Okay, well it looks like we need to begin doing some investigation of our own," she replied, looking at Cody.

"For what?" Tom asked, confused.

"I need to try to find Skylark's birthmother, to know with a surety that our adoption is legitimate. If she was stolen, she needs to be returned to her mother," Rachel replied matter-of-factly. "Thank you again for your help, Tom. It means the world. I don't want any other family to have to go through what we've been dealing with."

Tom looked perplexed, but shook Cody and her hand good-bye.

"Skylark's obviously with two good people," he said turning to leave. "I don't know that she'd be better off, but to each his own."

Rachel watched as he walked down the hall and disappeared into his uncle's office. She wrapped her arm around Cody's waist and he pulled her in for an exhausted, relieved embrace.

"Let's go home," she said.

***

190

Rachel looked up from her computer screen and stretched. She had only been at her Internet search for a little more than 30 minutes, but unsure of where to even begin, she was already defeated. With Skylark napping for another 20 minutes or so, and Cody working, she felt obligated to use the time to begin her search for Skylark's birth mother, but was at a loss for how to move forward.

Suddenly her phone rang.

"Susan," Rachel answered gratefully.

"Hey, girl!" Susan seemed to sing into the receiver. "I had a feeling I should call. How are things?"

Rachel laughed. "Well," she said hesitantly. "At this point it's all a matter of perspective. Let's just say I can see the light at the end of the tunnel...I think."

"Meet me for coffee? In an hour?"

"I'll be there."

***

Fall had officially arrived in Collinsville. The trees dotted along Main Street were outfitted with more golden and amber hues than green, and the light in the late morning sky was sharper and crisper. Skylark peered about from her carriage, her bright, big gray eyes sparkled as she took it all in.

Not only was Collinsville going through a seasonal transition, there was a spiritual shift in the air as well. Rachel's heart leapt as she passed *Watson's* and a college-aged guy was holding the door for an elderly couple. As she and Skylark approached *Cali's*, Rachel spotted Susan right away. Decked out in her brightest workout attire, there was no blending into the woodwork. Rachel smiled and waved and was greeted with Susan's brilliant white grin.

"Hey, girls!" she said embracing Rachel in a giant hug. She leaned over and gave Skylark a gentle kiss on the head. "I told Maddy you were on your way. She'll be out with your coffee..."

Before Susan was able to finish, Maddy was at the table

191

setting down a large mug of drip coffee with just the right amount of milk.

"Oh my gosh," Maddy exclaimed in a whisper. "She's even cuter than last week. Can I hold her? I just washed my hands."

"Of course," Rachel said, reaching in to hand Skylark to Maddy.

"Oh, Rach. She's amazing. She really has such a sweet, special spirit. It's like she was meant for you and Cody."

Maddy ran a finger lovingly along Skylark's hairline and then gently tucked her back in the carriage. "I would like to have one of those someday," she added with a wistful smile.

"Oh, Maddy!" Susan said. "That reminds me. There's a guy I'd like to introduce you to."

Rachel nearly spit out her coffee with laughter. "Subtle transition."

Susan rolled her eyes, but her cheeks went ever so slightly pink as she giggled.

"Well, in my world, looking to have a baby means you're first looking for a husband," she said, with a wink. "It's not a game of which came first, *the chicken or the egg*. Maddy's gonna need a chicken, well a handsome rooster, before she can have an egg, right?"

Both Maddy and Rachel were rolling with laughter, so much so that Skylark began to get slightly unnerved by the ruckus. Just as her lip turned down ready to start crying, Rachel pulled her out and cradled her softly against her chest.

"Thank you, Susan," Rachel said catching her breath. "I needed that. I haven't laughed like that in a long time."

Still giggling, Maddy turned to leave. "How's the coffee, Rachel? Do either of you need anything else?"

"Um," Rachel said, caught mid-sip. "It's delicious. I've actually been so sick with nerves lately I haven't had any coffee in nearly a week. I should slow down. I don't need to feel nauseous again."

"I'm sorry, Rach. That's horrible. Just wave if you need anything. I'll let you ladies talk," Maddy said. "Susan, I'd love to meet the handsome rooster sometime."

"I'll set something up. Thanks, girl."

Holding Skylark and rocking gently in her seat, Rachel basked in the warm, fuzzy feeling the sudden burst of laughter and caffeine had left her with.

"So, tell me, Rach. What's up? What's new with you?"

"Gosh, where do I begin?" Rachel wondered, realizing a lot had happened in the past couple of days. "Well, you know the moment you and I got home from our meeting with Tom, I'd started doing research, trying to find something that could be used as evidence. I was totally coming up blank. Then I had Melinda over. I saw it as an opportunity to try and share my feelings on things, to see if it might change her mind a bit, but it was also a chance for me to dig a little deeper. I needed to see if she had any new information."

Rachel paused to look around and lowered her voice.

"Out of nowhere she hands me a printout of an email between Zane, Uri, and their business partner in Croatia," she added. "It was totally incriminating them. Well, at least according to her, because it was in Croatian. It didn't matter though. She took the paper back, shoved it in her purse and we continued to chat. I tried to persuade her to make the right decision, but she was having none of it. I said goodbye, sad that I hadn't been persuasive enough and totally bummed that my only bit of evidence had walked out the door. Anyhow, *somehow* — it had to be divine intervention — the printout was left on the couch! Cody noticed it a little bit after Melinda left. I made copies and when she came back to retrieve it...I pretended I had no idea. As a side note, I'm a really good actress and it's not something I'm proud of."

Rachel took a deep breath. Susan was completely engrossed in the story. She waited with a look of astonishment as Rachel continued.

"So, Cody and I went to meet with the D.A. and Tom yesterday. It was a whirlwind. We took the train, then the subway, because we were both so tired from a nervous night's sleep. We didn't trust ourselves to drive. Then we went to the meeting. I was all prepared to formally present my findings. But, Matt just asked for the evidence, looked it over, and said if it panned out, they'd take action. I felt like I could've saved a trip and just texted it to him. But, it was good. Cody and I got a moment to talk to Tom after. He explained that since Matt's up for re-election…he's been looking for some good PR and breaking up a child laundering ring could be just what he needed. It's now in their hands."

Susan sat back and slapped her thighs in amazement. "I need to check in with you daily! This is incredible. So much has happened. What does this mean for Skylark?"

Rachel's heart sank and she held her daughter a little tighter.

"Well, I'm not sure. The D.A.'s not going to touch her unless there's a birthmother who comes forward with evidence that she's her daughter. The likelihood of that happening is basically zero. So, she's ours…but, I just can't feel good about it until I know without a doubt that her real mother put her up for adoption willingly. I can't selfishly keep Skylark if there's a mother out there missing her, praying for her return. I have to find her mom or something official that clearly shows she was put up for adoption legally. But again, my research is coming up completely blank. I don't even know where to begin on this one."

"Oh, sweetie, I can't believe how driven you are to do the right thing. I don't know if I'd be that strong," Susan replied.

"You would, too," Rachel countered, giving Susan's hand a pat. "Especially if you were looking to live up to the expectations of the little girl you loved more than you ever thought possible and she needed you to be her advocate and champion. You'd do everything in your power to be the best human you could possibly be; even if it meant breaking your own heart."

Susan was quiet for a moment, moved by what Rachel said.

"I have an idea," she said, suddenly inspired. "Brad Jensen…"

"The old man who sits in the back on Sundays?" Rachel asked, familiar with a rather grumpy, older gentleman from church by that name. She couldn't think of how he could possibly be of assistance.

"Yep," Susan replied cheerfully. "He was a spy in the 60s and 70s, and worked as a private investigator for a very long time after that. He only just retired a year or so ago. I bet he could help you find Skylark's birthmother. Or at least help guide your search."

"Really?" Rachel asked, surprised. "The same Brad Jensen who occasionally snores during the sermon?"

Susan laughed. "You're the one who said you didn't even know where to begin. I've given you a starting point…it may be a sleepy and grumpy starting point, but it's more than you had."

"It's true. I'll give him a call today," Rachel agreed. "There was something else I wanted to run by you."

"What is it?"

"Recently, it feels like all of my emotions are being dictated by outside forces. It's hard to explain, but it feels different. Most of the time, if I feel anxious or scared, happy or excited, it stems from how I internalize something or anticipate a situation to go; it very rarely is the environment or situation itself that influences my emotion," Rachel tried to explain, feeling like she was just confusing herself. "I don't know if I'm making any sense."

Susan leaned forward.

"Girl, you're totally making sense, and I think I know what it is," she said looking suddenly serious. "We're all

195

working very hard to fight for the light of Christ. Just like we've been battling through prayer to protect Collinsville, we need to pray for our own protection. With everything you've got going on in your life right now…and the fact that you're inspired, and determined, to choose to follow God and His plan for your life, makes the enemy very unhappy. He wants to cut you down. You've got to understand there's a constant battle all around us; quite literally a warring of good and evil. Just beyond the veil, beyond our conceptual awareness, angels and demons are fighting for dominion over people, places, and even things. Those external influences you're feeling are angels and demons fighting to have authority over you and lead you toward either light or darkness. You're not physically aware, but you're spiritually aware, and your body's picking up on that."

Rachel had *God bumps* up and down her arms. A soft chill ran down her spine and she shuddered, wishing for a warm hug or at the very least her cup of coffee to still be hot.

"That's so scary," she said. "In the midst of everything Cody and I are dealing with, you think we're also under spiritual attack?"

"Don't let it frighten you, sweetie. You're a chosen daughter of God. You've got angels on your side in droves," Susan said. "But, yes, it's exactly *because* of the situation you and Cody are dealing with that the enemy and his demons are working on you. You and Cody both have your hearts centered on Christ, but with your emotions raw and open, the enemy is looking for an opportunity to find a crack. He would like nothing more than to get two amazing, devoted, children of God to make a bad decision or justify a sin through his meddling influence during a time of difficulty."

"What can we do?" Rachel asked, concerned.

"We'll fast for you. We're planning a 40-day fast for Collinsville, assigning one family to fast per day. I'd like the first week to be a fast specifically for you and your family.

Not only do we all love you and want to protect you and Cody from spiritual attack, but I believe your efforts are key to clearing the darkness that's found its way into Collinsville. You're our champion, girl."

Rachel patted Susan's hand with gratitude. "It'd be so comforting to know we've got the congregation's support and prayers."

"If it's okay with you, Pastor Bishop and I will stop by after dinner...around 7 p.m.? We'd like to pray over your family for spiritual protection."

"I'd love that. Thank you. You always know what to do."

Susan smiled. "Well, I desire to have Holy Spirit as my constant companion. When He guides me, how could I be wrong?"

"I love that," Rachel said. "This was so nice to get out of the house and spend some time with you. Thank you for everything, really."

"Alrighty, girl. I'm gonna go hop on the phone and make sure we've got our families set up to fast for you. Expect us tonight."

"Will do. Since I'm here, I'm going to check up on the team. I haven't seen everyone in a few days."

Susan stood and bent over, wrapping her arms around Rachel in a strong embrace. "You're so strong. I'm so proud of you and I know God is so proud of you."

Rachel could feel her heart thump in her chest. It was the first time she had ever heard such a thing. It rang true in her heart and made her feel as though she might start crying. She felt an overwhelming sense of acceptance and love. At a lack for words, she simply nodded as Susan waved good-bye.

***

"Hello? Is this Brad Jensen?" Rachel asked, startled by the gruff voice on the other end of the line.

"Who's askin'?"

"This is Rachel Brooks, formerly D'Angelo, from

197

Collinsville Community Church. We've met a few times. I'm a 20-something brunette with long, straight hair."

"Ah. With the newborn from Croatia," he replied knowingly, his tone softening a bit.

"Yes. Did Susan mention I might call?"

"No. Haven't spoken to her since Sunday. You need a P.I.?" he asked not beating around the bush.

"Are you also telepathic?" Rachel asked with a laugh.

"It's the only reason people call me out of the blue."

Rachel felt a lump form in her throat. She felt terrible and was tempted to hang-up the phone.

"Don't feel bad. The Bible talks about talents," he added. "It's my talent. It's my service to mankind. Can't hide it… unless I need to do some espionage or something…then I'm quite expert at hiding it. Does it have something to do with your little girl?"

Feeling like a deer in headlights, Rachel managed to squeak out, "Yes."

"Happy to help."

***

Rachel stood over Skylark's crib watching her sleep. She wanted to bend over and kiss her forehead, but thought better of it not wanting to wake her.

"I love you," she whispered. After one last glance, she made her way down stairs to eat dinner with Cody.

"We have 30 minutes until the Bishops get here," she said walking up behind him at the stove. She wrapped her arms around his waist and giggled when she noticed he was wearing her frilly apron.

"What?" he asked jokingly. He handed her a plate with sautéed vegetables, grilled chicken and rice.

The exquisite plate of nutritious food Cody had thrown together after a full day of working on a commissioned armoire struck her in the chest. She set down the beautiful plate on the nicely set table and started crying.

"Rach?" he asked, concerned. "What is it?"

"I don't even know," she said through tears slumping into a chair. "I'm just so overwhelmed. You're so amazing and I feel like I'm failing! I don't even know how I got so lucky. I really feel like this whole ordeal is making me a terrible mom and horrible wife. I'm sorry."

Cody looked wounded. He knelt down before her and took her hands in his. "I totally understand why this is all getting to you. But, please, don't ever think you're failing or doing terribly at anything. You're incredible. If I get to help by occasionally making dinner, I'm grateful for the opportunity. I don't want you to do it all. I don't want you to feel like you have to do it all. Like I've said before, we're in this together."

Rachel dried her eyes and gave Cody a kiss. "I'm sorry. I think my body just needed to release some stress. I'm fine, really. I'm just really impressed with the level of kindness and love that's been freely given to us. I mean Susan, Tom, the members of the church, my employees at work, even Brad Jensen is helping us," she said. "You know him, right? The old, grumpy guy from church?"

Cody nodded. "Sure. He's actually really amazing," he started.

"Well, I had no idea," Rachel said. "But, I had an inspired conversation with him today and he's working to find Skylark's birth mom for us."

Just then Rachel's cellphone began to buzz.

"It's Tom," she said.

"Get it," Cody replied, eyes wide.

"Hello?" she answered putting it on speaker.

"They just picked up the Novaks," Tom said. "You're lead checked out."

"Where are they taking them?" Rachel asked, stunned.

"I believe to the Federal Corrections facility in Otisville. But, I'm not positive. I just wanted you to know before the

Collinsville rumor mill started."

"How'd you know about our rumor mill?" Rachel asked.

"Every small town has one," Tom replied. "They took everyone, including Melinda. Their son is currently with Child Protective Services. But, they will most likely release Melinda after questioning, as long as she really isn't involved."

Rachel's heart sank. "Is there anything we can do? To make Ivan more comfortable?"

"No," Tom said with a pause. "But, isn't this one of those times your Aunt would say a prayer? Maybe do that."

Rachel was dumbfounded by Tom's response and equally impressed. "That's perfect advice. Thank you. When will we know if Melinda gets released?"

"Within a day or two."

"Thank you, Tom. I really appreciate the call."

Rachel hung up and looked at Cody concerned.

"If this goes according to plan for Matt, this'll be all over the news soon," Rachel said. "Wait, it's almost 7 p.m. I bet he's going to have it strategically break in an hour, at 8 p.m. It'll be prime time. Nearly all of New York State will see that District Attorney Pierson is in the process of breaking up a child laundering crime ring…"

Rachel took a deep breath. "I have so many conflicting emotions right now. My head may explode."

"I really don't want that to happen," Cody said with a nervous chuckle. "I'm grateful the Bishop's are on their way over. We need them more than they even know. This is a circus that I don't naturally know how to handle."

"We aren't equipped for any of this. I don't know who would be. It would be impossible to handle without the help of Holy Spirit's guidance," Rachel said, her voice dropping with disbelief. "We should eat a little something. They'll be here any minute."

They each took a seat and meekly picked at the food. It

seemed to Rachel that most of their meals since Skylark's arrival had been purely out of sustenance as opposed to any form of enjoyment. Whether forcing down food for a lack of time, or appetite, or eating things cold that should be warm, or eating things lukewarm that should be cold; her days of being a foodie were on hold.

Just as they had eaten as much as they could stomach, there was a light knock at the door.

"Hello," Rachel said, greeting both Susan and Pastor Bishop with appreciative hugs. Taking their coats, she added, "We were both just talking about how we need this prayer even more than you know. Thank you for taking the time."

"What can I get you both to drink? We're like a well-stocked convenience store."

Pastor Bishop laughed. "I'll take some sort of sparkling water, if you have it."

"The same for me, please," Susan agreed.

As Cody went to the kitchen, Susan turned to Rachel. "Did something else happen since I last saw you?"

"As a matter of fact," Rachel started.

"Did it have anything to do with the entourage of black, government SUV's we saw leaving town just a few minutes ago?" Pastor Bishop asked. "They had beacon lights, similar to police, but not as large and no sirens."

"The Novaks were just picked up by the authorities on behalf of District Attorney Pierson," Rachel explained. "I have a feeling it will be on the news soon...you know, hit at primetime to ensure the most potential voters see what a good job he's doing at cleaning up crime. I feel a bit nauseous about the whole thing. Little Ivan's in with Child Protective Services until they release Melinda. That's *if* they release Melinda. Cody and I are both just feeling a little low. Especially since, at the moment, it's all mainly to benefit a politician's job security."

"Oh, sweetie," Susan said. "That's only the most visible

benefit. The Novaks being taken into custody, even Ivan going to Child Protective Services, is benefiting so many people and more lives than you can even imagine. It's truly even to the benefit of the Novaks, although I'm sure at the moment they'd beg to differ. The Lord is proud of you, Rach. You and Cody have both gone so far and above what most people, even well-meaning people, would do. You and I already talked about that this morning, but, honestly, any doubts or remorse you're feeling is the work of darkness. It is Satan who leverages our own self-doubts and fears to push us off-track of doing the right thing or stall us from completing God's work."

"You always have the best answers," Rachel said. "Thank you."

Cody handed the Bishops their drinks and gave Rachel a glass of water.

"Let's get started, shall we?" Pastor Bishop asked.

He directed everyone to kneel on the floor and hold hands.

"Dear Heavenly Father, we come before you this evening as your children, full of faith and trust in your Holy word. We ask for a spiritual blessing for Cody, Rachel, and their daughter, Skylark. As they do Your work, as they strive to do right and find Skylark's birthmother, cleanse Collinsville of all darkness, and save other families from the Novaks' illegal adoptions, we ask that You safeguard them from evil," Pastor Bishop prayed. Rachel could feel the warmth of divine electricity running through their hands. Holy Spirit was with them. "Let Holy Spirit and your blessed Angels be with them to guard, protect, and guide them in their efforts. Bless their home with your Spirit, Lord. Please bless Cody and Rachel with steadfast faith and unwavering focus in their work for You, Dear Lord. We love you and believe in Your almighty power to offer them security against the adversary and his spirit of darkness. We love and praise you in Jesus' name, Amen!"

CHAPTER TWELVE
A BIRTHDAY SURPRISE

Rachel rocked in the chair slowly, full of love and emotion as she watched Skylark's sleepy eyes droop closed even though she was still nursing hungrily at the bottle. Not only had Rachel felt her own spirit strengthen since the Bishops' visit, she had felt the spirit of the home brighten over the past week. She felt surrounded by beautiful blessings, Holy Spirit, friends, and family.

Whether it was the knowledge that people were fasting and praying for them throughout the week or the divine love and protection their prayers delivered, Rachel's nerves had relinquished and she was full of faith; even though her nausea continued to linger. Even as she checked in with Brad Jensen throughout the week, she had a sense of peace, no matter what his findings; of which there were few.

He had gained a solid lead from the nurse that had been paid to transport Skylark from Croatia. She had provided the name of a woman who was supposed to be friends with Skylark's birthmother. Through the grapevine, they discovered that she was possibly a young college student and practicing Catholic. When she discovered she was pregnant, the only thing that made sense was adoption. But, even with the nurse's firsthand account, Mr. Jensen was finding it challenging to pursue the lead any further.

"It's a tough case when the key witness can't tell us

anything," he had said the last time they spoke. Thinking of Skylark as a witness, and potential victim, had left Rachel feeling especially protective of her little girl.

She gave Skylark a reassuring squeeze and then tucked her into the baby wrap and stood to double-check the diaper bag.

"Okay, my love," Rachel whispered, giving her a kiss on the forehead. "Let's go."

As she reached the bottom of the stairs, Cody was waiting for them. "You ready?" he asked gently, seeming concerned.

"Yes," she replied confidently.

They started the short walk to town, down the long gravel driveway, holding hands. In their comfortable silence, Rachel paid attention to the sound of gravel crunching beneath her shoes and how Cody's heavy work boots tended to pick up rocks in their thick tread and kick them out as he walked. It would be dinnertime when they got back, she thought, and wondered whether they should just eat out after their meeting. She decided if it was good news they would go out. It would be like a celebration. If it wasn't good news, they would just go home.

"I'm eager to hear what he's found," she said, her voice seeming loud in the stillness of the late afternoon. "I'm hopeful it's in line with the lead he found earlier this week; but, of course, concerned he's found something unexpected. I don't know…what do they say in the military? Hope for the best, prepare for the worst? I'm trying to do that."

Cody smiled and looked at her sweetly with his big green eyes. "Do they say that in the military?" he asked. "I've heard it, but wasn't familiar with where it came from. Are you nervous at all? I'm nervous. More nervous than I expected to be."

"Yes, I am too," Rachel admitted. "I know he's found something big, otherwise he would've just gone over everything on the phone or at church on Sunday."

As they rounded the corner to Main Street, she took a deep breath and felt a soft breeze blow past comforting her. She squeezed Cody's hand, hoping he noticed it, too.

"He's already there," she said, spotting Mr. Jensen sitting at a table in front of *Cali's*.

They picked up their pace and just as they went to greet him, Cody grabbed Rachel's arm. "I love you," he said. "I love Skylark. We're a family no matter what he says."

"I love you and I know Skylark does, too. We *are* a family. The Lord has brought us together for a purpose and no matter what we find out about Skylark's birthmother, we've entered into, gone through, and will emerge from this craziness together, as a family," Rachel replied with a smile.

"Hello, Mr. Jensen," she said extending a hand. "I hope you weren't waiting long."

"No, no," he said, standing to shake her and Cody's hands. "Not at all. I got here early for coffee and to people watch. There are few things I enjoy more as a retired P.I. than people watching. It's great fun to guess at who's meeting whom, and for what, or what sort of day people are having. When I was here a month or so ago, it was astonishing how many people were having a bad day. Today, it appears most people are in very good spirits."

"How can you tell?" Rachel asked, getting situated in her seat.

"It's all in their body language," he said. "Plus, I can read lips."

"Wow," Rachel exclaimed. "That's incredible, and good to know. Just another reason to make sure I speak kindly of others!"

They all laughed.

"Did you two want to get a drink before we begin?" he asked.

"I'm too anxious for coffee," Rachel answered. "Cody? How about you?"

"Maybe after we talk," he agreed.

"Well," Mr. Jensen started in. "The lead from the nurse ended up panning out. I received a call in the middle of the night from a woman by the name of Ana Markovic. I don't think she realized that although it was 9 a.m. her time, it was 3 a.m. for me. She was very soft spoken, which for an old man can be a bit of a challenge, especially at such an hour, but her English was good and we had an enlightening conversation. There's no need to delay the news. Cody, Rachel, I believe Ana is Skylark's birthmother. I don't have any reason to suspect that someone is trying to cover anything up or mislead us. Her story matched up with the nurse. Plus, her account of how she got involved with the orphanage also makes sense and provides a bit more fodder for your friend, District Attorney Pierson."

Rachel was speechless. It was what she had hoped for, but hearing it was incredible. "I want you to tell us everything," she said. "But, just to be sure I'm hearing you right, Ana willingly put Skylark up for adoption? The adoption is legal?"

"Yes," he said, something catching in his throat. After a bout of coughing, he added, "She explained the only reason she called was to make sure the baby was with a nice American family, like she had agreed to. She had become skeptical and worried about the child, because of how the adoption was handled by *CTB*. She was relieved and grateful to hear a little about you two. And, after telling me everything about Skylark's birth, she asked to never be contacted again. Which, I feel we should respect."

"Oh, my goodness," Rachel said. "Oh, thank you."

Looking at Cody, feeling Skylark shift in the wrap snug against her chest, she felt warmth radiate from her heart throughout her entire body.

"She's our girl," she said. "For real. She really was meant for us. She's ours."

Cody lifted a hand and placed it gently against Skylark,

tears welling in eyes.

"Oh, man," he said. "Amen to that. And, good riddance to this chapter of our lives."

Rachel gave Cody a wholehearted smile. Turning to Mr. Jensen, she asked again to confirm, "You're sure? With all of your expertise, you really believe this was Skylark's mom? And, she really wants Skylark to be with us?"

The man she had formerly viewed as an embittered miser, smiled. He cleared his throat again, this time seemingly from a bout of emotion, and nodded. "Yes, dear. It checks out both factually, logically, but also in my gut…which has seldom led me off target."

Cody put his arm around Rachel's shoulders and brought her and Skylark just a little closer to him.

"Tell us about her," he said. "Tell us how Skylark ended up with the Novaks."

"Like we'd heard through the nurse, Ana is a young college student. Very young; 17. She's advanced in her studies, but not in the ways of the world. A devout Catholic, she made a couple of poor choices with her boyfriend and when she found out she was pregnant, adoption was her only option. From the moment she found out, she started praying for guidance on where to go for help. Then one day, after praying in a bathroom stall at school, she came across a flyer for a fertility center. The flyer advertised a big paycheck for college girls interested in selling their eggs, and at the very bottom there was a note about help for girls with unwanted pregnancies. She called the number and they sent her to the *CTB International* agency in Croatia. She didn't decide to work with them though until the very end of her pregnancy. Right after finalizing all of the paperwork, she went into labor early. Which ultimately worked for them. They were accustom to transporting babies with their nurse, so they just had the nurse pick up Skylark from the hospital as opposed to the orphanage."

Rachel had to stifle tears, she was so grateful. "Skylark never even spent time in an orphanage. She went straight from the hospital with her mom to us," she reiterated, filled with relief. Then, fear swooped in again and she asked, "But, from what Melinda's told me, and what you are saying, this nurse is one of their key players. Why was she so willing to talk to you?"

"I made it clear we were only looking to connect with the birthmother. I didn't ask her to say anything against her employers or tell me anything that could put her job in jeopardy. Although I did let her know that she might not be getting any new work from them anytime soon and offered to make it worth her while. Knowing she might not see another payday from them, she was happy to oblige."

Rachel smiled. "I'm sorry. I just can't believe this is real. I don't think I've ever been so happy and grateful."

Mr. Jensen smiled again. "The Novaks have been running a questionable practice, but your little Skylark's adoption process was legitimate," he concluded. "The one thing that throws me, is, it seems the Novaks may also be running a fertility center."

"We'll let Rachel's contact, Tom, know," Cody replied.

Squeezing Skylark gently and kissing her forehead, Rachel held Cody's hand tightly.

"Thank you so much, Mr. Jensen. You have brought our family so much peace, unity, and certainty. I don't think we'll ever be able to repay you."

"No need, my dear," he said. "And, please, call me Brad."

***

Rachel ran her fingers over the beautiful hand embroidery on the white, silk baby gown.

"Isn't it the sweetest thing you've ever seen?" Maddy asked, pulling out the accompanying bonnet.

"It's precious, and so perfect," Rachel replied. "It will be beautiful on Skylark this Sunday. What do you think? Should we start carrying baby items?"

"Definitely!" Maddy replied excitedly. "We could dedicate a corner to a little baby section. Although, it could be dangerous...you should see the adorable things some of our women's vendors carry for babies."

Rachel laughed, worried at the thought. "Ooh. That could be dangerous, actually. I might make this place rich, while personally bankrupting myself...not sure what that would mean. We'll have to think about it. Plus, I don't know where we would put one more item."

Looking around the backroom of *Cali's Closet*, they both laughed. It was jam packed with new inventory in preparation for holiday shopping. With October just days away, they were gearing up for their busiest season at both the cafe and boutique.

Bells chimed from the front door, and Rachel could hear a chorus of voices calling her. She looked at Maddy for clarification, who just smiled and winked. "Sounds like you're wanted out front."

Curious, Rachel made her way to find Cody holding Skylark, Susan, Pastor Bishop, Brad Jensen, Teresa and her daughters, a handful of other friends from church, and all of her employees gathered together around a lit birthday cake, singing loudly.

Rachel began to giggle with surprise. She had forgotten it was her birthday altogether.

Greeting Cody with a kiss, she leaned forward and blew out all 28 candles. As Susan cut the cake and Maddy handed out slices paired with *Watson's* cheesecake yogurt, Rachel made the rounds thanking everyone personally for such a nice surprise. There was something wonderfully heartening about her friends and loved ones remembering such a personal day, that she herself had forgotten.

"What a surprise," Rachel whispered to Cody. "I honestly forgot, but you all remembering has made it one of the most lovely surprises ever. I've been so busy after everything with the Novaks. Getting back to work, taking Skylark to the mommy and me activities, getting ready for her dedication, and volunteering again, I've just lost track…of me, I guess."

Cody put his hand around her waist. "And, that's why you're on your way to *Bella's Spa* for some pampering. Then we're going out for a romantic dinner. Susan insisted on watching Skylark."

"Yep," Susan said, joining their conversation. "I can't wait to get a night of cuddling in with that little angel."

"You guys," Rachel hemmed. "This is so nice, but so unnecessary."

"Happy Birthday, girl. Just enjoy," Susan said.

"You're appointment's at noon, starting with a massage, so you should start wrapping up here soon," Cody added. "I'll meet you at *Francesco's* at 6 p.m."

"Thank you all so much," Rachel said, feeling surrounded by love and support.

***

Laying in the sauna, feeling relaxed and rejuvenated from her massage, Rachel took a deep breath of the steamy eucalyptus-scented air. She felt as though the dark, difficult chapter of the Novaks had finally closed. She could physically feel a difference in her heart, mind, and body.

Just the day before, Rachel had finally gotten the opportunity to go and make her peace with Melinda. After waiting for the dust to settle and see where Melinda landed in the midst of the case against the Novaks, Rachel received a call from Tom letting her know that she was returning to Collinsville to pick up some of her personal belongings.

After intensive questioning, the federal authorities released her to the custody of her sister who lived in a nice New Jersey suburb. Because of her involvement, Melinda was on house arrest, ankle bracelet and all. But she and Ivan were together, and they were with family.

Tom had called to give Rachel the head's up that Melinda would be returning to Collinsville for a very small window of time. Ankle bracelet already attached, the road trip from New Jersey to Collinsville and back was being tracked and timed by authorities. Rachel found the opportunity with restrictions somewhat comforting, as she wouldn't have to stay too long.

Walking up the familiar path to Melinda's Collinsville dream home, purchased less than six months prior, Rachel felt momentarily sorrowful recalling the story Uri and Melinda had told when they first met at the agency in the city. He and Melinda had both talked wistfully of the goal they had to one day own a big home in the country with lots of children. It was that dream that had prompted Rachel to invite them out to visit Collinsville in the first place.

Looking at the beautiful home they had achieved with a spacious front lawn and sprawling property, she considered how they had almost attained what they said they wanted. Saddened by the memory, disappointed she had been unable to persuade Melinda to talk to Uri, she hesitated at the steps up to the front porch.

Rachel felt culpable for the Novaks' predicament and wondered if she would be able to face Melinda without wearing guilt across her countenance.

Suddenly, a gentle breeze swept past, warming Rachel and providing her with a sense of compassion overwhelming any sense of sadness or shame. A still, small voice recited a familiar Bible verse in her heart.

For what will it profit a man if he gains the whole world, and loses his own soul? Or what will a man give in exchange for his soul? Mark 8:36-37.

Rachel smiled at the reminder. The Novaks had corrupted their own dreams as a result of earthly greed. Whether influenced by Uri's parents, or each of them through their own self-justification of petty sins, the Novaks had made their bed; regardless of whether Rachel sped up the process or not.

Ultimately, they still had time to start putting stock in their Heavenly profit. Rachel prayed their fall would result in some positive soul-searching. Then, feeling a little better, she approached the door.

Standing at the door she was overcome with a dark feeling she hadn't experienced in weeks. It was reminiscent of when she heard the man shouting at the children's soccer game or when she found out that *Watson's* had failed the health inspection. She stepped back unsure whether she should stay.

I am with you always, the voice emanating from her heart replied.

Knocking softly, she was greeted by a woman who looked very little like Melinda.

"Hello," she said looking at Rachel inquisitively.

"Hi. I'm Rachel Brooks. I heard that Melinda might be here."

"She is. I'm her sister, Nessa," she offered a hand and then turned to shout up the stairs. "Lin! You got company. Rachel Brooks!"

Melinda appeared at the top of the stairs and paused momentarily, seeming to decide whether or not to come down. After a beat she made her way to meet Rachel at the door.

"I was hoping I could speak with you for a few minutes," Rachel asked, waiving her outside in the hopes she wouldn't have to go in, as the darkness she felt at the door seemed to be pervasive throughout the interior.

Melinda joined her on the patio closing the door behind her.

"So, I guess you heard? Everyone's in jail," she said, taking a seat on the steps.

"Yes," Rachel replied, sitting next to her.

"Do you want to say, 'I told you so'?"

"No."

Melinda looked Rachel in the eyes and offered a weak smile. "You were right. I just decided I agreed a bit too late."

"What do you mean?"

"I actually had a talk with Uri the night before federal agents came to pick us all up. He was preparing to tell his dad he wanted out," Melinda said with a laugh. "I should have listened to you. I should have said something to everyone. It ends up, everyone was wanting to put an end to it...it's just nobody said anything...nobody wanted to disappoint the other. But, everyone's true feelings have come to light since we've been questioned for hours on end. Funny how things work."

"I'm sorry to hear that," Rachel said. "Do you know anything about when the official trial will be?"

"No, not yet," she sighed. "It seems like all of the lawyers are pushing for a delay. The guys fighting for us want to push it, so that the public forgets a bit...it's been all over the news. The guys fighting for the state want to push it so that the trial hits after the D.A.'s been re-elected. My guess is late November."

"They aren't allowed out on bond?" Rachel asked.

"Maybe in the future. Not yet, though. They're still trying to untangle everything tied to Croatia. Zane and his business partners, as well as Uri most likely, have also been tied to a fertility center as well. It may have been adding to the child laundering. So, they're staying put for a while. I am just in shock. Pretty numb about the whole thing, really. I'm just so relieved to be with Ivan and that my sister and her family are willing to take us in."

Unsure of how to respond, Rachel offered a smile. "Hopefully it'll be a better experience than living with your in-laws. And, you'll be close to where Uri is, right? You can go and visit?"

"Yeah," Melinda said, sounding distant.

Turning to look out at the beautiful fall landscape before them, almost all of the trees having transitioned from green to golden, Rachel considered what to say.

"I just heard you were here and wanted to let you know that I was thinking of you. Is there anything I can do for you and Ivan?" she asked.

"No. We'll be fine," Melinda said. "Thank you, Rachel. You've been a good friend. You've always been willing to hear me out and you tried. In retrospect, you tried *very* hard to help me make the right decision."

"Is there any chance Uri will get released?"

"I don't think so," Melinda said. "It's going to be a long road. Not really the life I envisioned for myself. Definitely not what Uri imagined. He's so disappointed in himself. But, you know, there's this strange sense of relief with everyone…like we don't have to keep up the lies anymore."

Melinda stopped and shrugged. "It is what it is," she added. "I should get back inside. I've only got an hour here. We need to be back to Jersey by 5 p.m."

"Take care, Melinda," Rachel said, standing.

"You too," Melinda replied, giving her a small, sideways hug.

Rachel smiled and made her way down the stairs. Feeling a dark chapter in her life close as she walked toward the street, she decided to not look back. A weight lifted off her shoulders as she heard the door close behind her.

On her walk back home, Rachel had felt prompted to call Tom and thank him for all of the extra effort. His insider information had allowed her and Cody to truly move past the challenging experience and enjoy their new life as parents.

"Yes?" he said, picking up the phone.

"I just finished meeting with Melinda and wanted to say thanks. You really didn't have to give me the head's up; but it was a good conversation and is going to help me move on from all of this," Rachel said. "Thank you, Tom."

He was quiet.

"That's it. I just wanted to say thank you," she reiterated.

"You're welcome," he replied. There was something in his

voice leading Rachel to believe he needed something.

"I'd like to repay the favor," she blurted out, unexpectedly. "Is there anything I can do for you?"

"Well," he said, hesitantly. "I wasn't going to say anything, but I'm wondering if you might offer some guidance on how to research the text in the Bible."

Rachel's tongue felt as if it swelled three sizes. It felt fat and clumsy with surprise.

"For a case?" she asked.

"No," he replied, sounding embarrassed. "For personal reasons. I only ask because I started reading last night and I didn't get what all the fuss is about."

"You started to read? On page one?" she had asked.

"Yes," he said, matter-of-factly. "It's a book, right?"

Knowing Tom, she didn't want to mess up the opportunity to share the Lord's word with him. She said a silent prayer for guidance, the ability to quote scripture, offer advice on a study guide, anything that might bring him to know God.

Invite him to the dedication.

"What're you doing Sunday?" she asked.

Reminiscing about the conversation made her smile. She couldn't believe he had accepted. Looking about *Bella's* sauna, she was so grateful it was quiet and, for the moment, just her. The soft, meditative music playing and privacy of the empty room had her in a dreamy state. As she happily thought about Skylark and Cody spending the afternoon together, she wondered what they were doing. Her mind wandered from the two of them, to her gratitude for her 28th year. If she had known the twists and turns life would throw at her when she was six, she probably would have huddled in a corner. But, she had made it through with the help of Holy Spirit, and she would make it through so much more with His divine support in the future.

"But, not too much more, please?" she asked softly, hopeful.

Smiling, she resolved to be completely aware of the joy and peace she had in this moment. She couldn't be happier than she was with her life right now. But she wanted to give Skylark a sibling sooner rather than later. Considering going through the adoption process again made her heart flutter with nerves. She feared she had ruined her reverie, but the thought came and went. She found she was able to ponder the thought without any deeper anxiety.

As she embraced how much her personal strength had grown through her spiritual faith, she felt empowered. Contemplating this evolution she found herself absentmindedly rubbing her belly. It was an odd thing to do, she thought. Then realizing the date, September 27, she gasped. The month had completely escaped her.

She was way overdue for her period.

Sitting up, suddenly very present, she realized it had been more than a month.

"No way," she whispered to herself.

Grabbing her towel she went to get her purse. Fishing through the various odds and ends that had found their way in to her once organized bag since becoming a mom. She dug down for one of the pregnancy tests she had stashed at the beginning of the year. During her baby crazy phase, prior to deciding to adopt, Rachel had been buying pregnancy tests in bulk. Tucked away in a side pocket, buried beneath baby formula packs and a pacifier, Rachel found a test stick.

Stunned at the mere consideration of a pregnancy, she put her purse away and made her way to the ladies room.

***

"You look stunning," Cody said, greeting her at the front of *Francesco's*.

"I'm so relaxed, I might fall asleep in my spaghetti," she said with a giggle. "*Bella's* went above and beyond. Massage, sauna, facial, blowout, makeup, the works. I feel like a shiny new penny."

Cody laughed. "I would like to say something about *more like a million bucks*, but I won't. That's too cheesy for me, even."

"That's pretty cheesy," she agreed giving him a kiss. "I'll take it, though."

"Our table's all ready. Should we head in?"

Cody led her to a charming table outside under glowing globe lights and a clear, crisp fall sky, dotted with seemingly endless stars. Votive candles sparkled from the top of the table. Pulling out her chair, Cody held her hand as she took a seat.

"I always feel like a city girl when I get a chance to appreciate the stars in Collinsville. I never get used to them," she said. "They're totally awe inspiring; like a glimpse into Heaven."

Cody nodded.

"It feels weird to be out, just the two of us," he said. "It's strange to be out together and not need to discuss some life-altering issue."

Rachel laughed.

"Can you believe it's been a year since we were here for our groom's dinner?" she asked, looking around. "It was warmer this time last year."

"Yeah, *someone* gave us a very nice wedding gift of unseasonably warm weather," he said with a smile. "It's been an interesting first year, huh?"

"Has it ever," she sighed. Taking sip of water and contemplating for a moment, she added, "But, you know, we did it. We never got a honeymoon period. We were confronted with some really difficult stuff from the very beginning. We were dealing with challenges on all fronts...even spiritual, and together we made it."

He smiled. "We're a great team. What I like to think of as a match made in Heaven."

Cody grimaced at his own joke and kissed her hand.

Rachel laughed and ran her fingers along his strong jawline.

"We should make this a priority while we can," she said. "The two of us getting out. We should try to do a date night once a week. I love just being able to look at you without distractions."

"Sounds like a plan," he said.

Suddenly a waiter appeared with salads and breadsticks.

"Ooh, my favorite," Rachel cooed. "They have the best house dressing here."

"Let's eat, birthday girl."

***

"Shall we go for a walk?" he asked, signing the check. "The park?"

"You read my mind," she said.

He put his jacket over her shoulders and took her hand in his. She nestled under his arm as they walked in the cold night air. The moon and stars made the path sparkle and completely illuminated the lake as they entered.

"It feels like God's light has returned to Collinsville," she said. "It feels pure here again, special…not caught up in things of this world."

"It was a long, dark summer," he agreed. "But, you can tell there's something special brewing for winter. It's going to be an amazing holiday season. Everything feels completely lit up and electric."

"Skylark's going to love jack-o-lanterns and Christmas lights. Oh, I can't wait to share it all with her," Rachel said with excitement.

"This really is such a great place to raise a kid," Cody said. "I'm so grateful to be here, doing this with you, Rach. You're an amazing mom and such a strong woman of faith. Skylark's such a lucky girl. I'm such a lucky guy."

She blushed. "Ditto."

"I'm hesitant to say anything," he said. "But, should we

start looking into adopting again? I'd like to give Skylark a sibling."

Rachel could tell he was nervous to even bring it up. "After all we've been through?" she asked smiling. "You'd be willing to do it again?"

"Sure," he said. "For her, for you, for all of us. I believe God has more kids for us."

Rachel guided him to her favorite bench and they took a seat. Suddenly a star shot across the sky.

"Did you see that?" Cody asked.

"Yes. It was beautiful."

"Make a wish," he said, wrapping his arm around her and drawing her in.

Rachel rested her head on his shoulder, sinking into his embrace. "I've already gotten my wish," she said softly.

The air was still around them, as if all of Collinsville was holding its breath.

Lifting her lips to his ear, she whispered tenderly, "I'm pregnant."

He turned, taking her hands in his. "Pregnant?" he repeated with a note of wonder and surprise.

Rachel nodded and gazed intently into his eyes, feeling so blessed. In the soft autumn moonlight she spotted a rogue tear rolling down Cody's cheek. "That's a...," he swallowed, working to keep the flood of emotion hitting him at bay.

"It's a miracle," Rachel said softly.

A gentle breeze blew past, like a soft exhale, wiping at Rachel's hair.

Cody wrapped his hands around her face and pulled her forehead to his. The warmth of his face and breath brought an overwhelming sense of peace and togetherness. She lifted her head, and staring into his eyes, filled with joy, she could feel a blessed energy encircle them. Another soft breeze blew past, causing the fall leaves to rustle in a sort of applause of their union, and she knew Holy Spirit was with them.

Cody leaned forward and embraced her fully. As his lips met hers, she was filled with a current of divine electricity. Unified in love and faith, she could feel her heart and soul expanding, filled with gratitude for Heavenly Father, Cody's love, Skylark, and their unborn child, she rested her head against his chest.

"Family," Cody said dreamily. "I love you, Rach."

"And I love you, Mr. Brooks."

"Once your physical eyes are open to spiritual truth, the pathway for Supernatural can begin."

— Tammy Hotsenpiller

TEN STEPS TO TAKE WHEN
YOU ARE UNDER SPIRITUAL ATTACK

Step One: Know Who Your Enemy *Is* and Who It Is Not

We do not wrestle against flesh and blood, but against principalities and powers in unseen places. Don't assume your loved ones, friends, or colleagues are your enemy. The real warfare is to be fought with Satan. Jesus won that battle for you already.

Step Two: Prayer Walk

This is one of the best ways to focus and hear from God. There is something about motion and prayer that help me to connect with Holy Spirit. As I walk and cry out to God, my spirit bears witness with His Spirit and before long I have clarity and perspective for my request.

Step Three: Fast

Fasting has become a regular part of my life. Once I understood the power of fasting I began to see my prayer life go to a new level. Think of fasting as warfare.

Every time my stomach begins to growl, I go into a time of intercession and conversation with God. I am doing battle with the enemy and reminding him of the power of my prayer. Jesus said, "Some things only happen by prayer and fasting."

Step Four: Get Counsel From a Reliable Source

Having someone to talk with and give you godly counsel is key in managing spiritual attacks. Often we get overwhelmed and side-tracked by the ploys of darkness. Having wise counsel will keep you focused on how to move into the realm of the Spirit of God.

Step Five: Read the Word of God

This step is imperative. The Word of God is your roadmap from the Father's heart. By reading and meditating on God's word you bring light and life to your circumstances. *"Thy Word is a lamp unto my feet and a light unto my path."*

Step Six: Fill Your Mind with Truth

Listen to Biblical teachings, worship music, and podcasts. With all the online resources we have today this is an easy step to take. Fill your heart and mind with the Word of God and good instruction. You can check out my podcast at TammyHotsenpiller.com.

Step Seven: Memorize Scripture

The best way to fight the enemy is with the Word of God. Three times Jesus battled Satan with scripture when He was assaulted. The enemy can't stand up to God's Word. *"Thy Word have I hid in my heart that I might not sin against Thee."* See list of scripture on page 227.

Step Eight: Remember This is Just a Season

Your breakthrough is on its way. Warfare comes in seasons and will not last forever. By knowing how to do battle you can short-circuit the enemy's plans for your life. Begin to see yourself as more than a conqueror. You are victorious. You have already won.

Step Nine: Don't Talk with the Enemy, Talk to the Enemy

Don't give the Enemy space in your head or your behavior. This step is one that takes time and discipline. We are by nature "stinking thinkers." Our mind naturally goes toward what can go wrong. But when you put on the mind of Christ you begin to see your battle though the eyes of God. The Bible tells us in Philippians 4:8 that we are to *think* on certain things.

The list goes like this: *Whatever things are true, whatever things are noble, whatever things are right, whatever is pure, whatever is lovely, whatever is admirable, if anything is excellent or praiseworthy — think on these things.*

Think on these things. God wants to rewire our mind to think as He thinks. When you begin to think your warfare is bigger than your victory, it's time to take the Philippians' test.

Step Ten: Get Enough Rest and Exercise

This may seem odd as a defense against the enemy but in truth it is very important. When Elijah was running from Jezebel, the Angel of the Lord told him to rest and eat. Often we are so physically and emotionally exhausted that we can't fight off the lies of the enemy.

ADDENDUM: SCRIPTURE
TO BATTLE SPIRITUAL WARFARE

"Be self-controlled and alert. Your enemy the devil prowls around like a roaring lion looking for someone to devour. Resist him, standing firm in the faith." 1 Peter 5:8-9

"Submit yourselves to God. Resist the devil, and he will flee from you." James 4:7

"Put on the full armor of God, so that you can take your stand against the devil's schemes. For our struggle is not against flesh and blood, but against the rulers, against the authorities, against the powers of this dark world and against the spiritual forces of evil in the heavenly realms. Therefore put on the full armor of God, so that when the day of evil comes, you may be able to stand your ground, and after you have done everything, to stand. Stand firm then, with the belt of truth buckled around your waist, with the breastplate of righteousness in place, and with your feet fitted with the readiness that comes from the gospel of peace. In addition to all this, take up the shield of faith, with which you can extinguish all the flaming arrows of the evil one. Take the helmet of salvation and the sword of the Spirit, which is the word of God." Ephesians 6:11-17

"You are from God, little children, and have overcome them; because greater is He who is in you than he who is in the world." 1 John 4:4

"Behold, I have given you authority to tread on serpents and scorpions, and over all the power of the enemy, and nothing shall hurt you." Luke 10:19

"For though we live in the world, we do not wage war as the world does. The weapons we fight with are not the weapons of the world. On the contrary, they have divine power to demolish strongholds. We demolish arguments and every pretension that sets itself up against the knowledge of God, and we take captive every thought to make it obedient to Christ." 2 Corinthians 10:3-5

"'Not by might nor by power, but by My Spirit,' says the Lord of hosts." Zechariah 4:6

"'No weapon that is formed against you will prosper; and every tongue that accuses you in judgment you will condemn. This is the heritage of the servants of the Lord, and their vindication is from Me,' declares the Lord." Isaiah 54:17

"Truly I tell you, whatever you bind on earth will be bound in heaven, and whatever you loose on earth will be loosed in heaven. Again, truly I tell you that if two of you on earth agree about anything they ask for, it will be done for them by my Father in heaven." Matthew 18:18-19

"In all these things, we are more than conquerors through Him who loved us." Romans 8:37

"The thief comes only to steal and kill and destroy. I came that they may have life and have it abundantly." John 10:10

"I have told you these things, so that in me you may have peace. In this world you will have trouble. But take heart! I have overcome the world." John 16:33

"But thanks be to God, who gives us the victory through our Lord Jesus Christ." 1 Corinthians 15:57

"But the Lord is faithful, and he will strengthen you and protect you from the evil one." 2 Thessalonians 3:3

"But they who wait for the Lord shall renew their strength; they shall mount up with wings like eagles; they shall run and not be weary; they shall walk and not faint." Isaiah 40:31

"What then shall we say to these things? If God is for us, who is against us?" Romans 8:31

"And they have conquered him by the blood of the Lamb and by the word of their testimony, for they loved not their lives even unto death." Revelation 12:11

"The Lord will cause your enemies who rise against you to be defeated before you. They shall come out against you one way and flee before you seven ways." Deuteronomy 28:7

"Do not be overcome with evil, but overcome evil with good." Romans 12:21

"Do not fear them, for the Lord your God is the one fighting for you." Deuteronomy 3:22

"No temptation has overtaken you except what is common to mankind. And God is faithful; he will not let you be tempted beyond what you can bear. But when you are tempted, he will also provide a way out so that you can endure it." 1 Corinthians 10:13

"For You have girded me with strength for battle; You have subdued under me those who rose up against me." Psalms 18:39

"And you will know the truth, and the truth will set you free." John 8:32

"He who dwells in the shelter of the Most High will rest in the shadow of the Almighty. I will say of the Lord, He is my refuge and my fortress, my God, in whom I trust. Surely he will save you from the fowler's snare and from the deadly pestilence. He will cover you with his feathers, and under his wings you will find refuge; his faithfulness will be your shield and rampart..." Psalms 91:1-4

"Fight the good fight of the faith. Take hold of the eternal life to which you were called when you made your good confession in the presence of many witnesses." 1 Timothy 6:12